CLACKAMAS LITERARY REVIEW

2026
Volume XXX

Clackamas Community College
Oregon City, Oregon

CLACKAMAS LITERARY REVIEW

Cover Art

Blue-Eyed Darner by Carina Cooper

The Clackamas Literary Review is published annually at Clackamas Community College. Manuscripts are read from September 1st to December 31st. By submitting your work to *CLR*, you indicate your consent for us to publish accepted work in print and online. Issues I–XI are available through our website; issues XII–XXIX are available on our Submittable, and through your favorite online bookseller.

Clackamas Literary Review
19600 Molalla Avenue, Oregon City, Oregon 97045
ISBN: 978-1-7320333-8-2
Printed by Lightning Source
www.clackamasliteraryreview.org

CONTENTS

EDITORS' NOTE

POETRY

PROSE

POSSIBILITY

CONTRIBUTORS

Editors' Note

Here. Please, *sit—*

There's a place for you at this table.

We've been preparing everything for quite some time now—sorting through the harvest, taste-testing ingredients, charting brand-new flavor combinations, and reinventing familiar ones.

As first-time chefs, it's been an enlightening, bordering on slightly terrifying, experience; the dread of sharing an unsuccessful recipe is compounded, and then compounded *again* by our sincerest desire to impress your palate. But it's through this adversity, this honest-to-god fear of failure, that we've also realized something about ourselves—this direct confrontation with the unsavory is what has been the biggest motivator in our growth. And it's for this reason that we dedicate this buffet:

To those who have yet to dispel the aftertaste of grief, following the sweet dollop of daring-to-love; to those who have felt the weight of a world that never cared to slow down; to those who know loss intimately, in all of its many flavors—for anyone who has never quite felt like they've "gotten over it."

Because maybe getting over it *isn't the point.* Maybe there's purpose in sitting with the sanguine, the melancholy, and all the bittersweet in-betweens. Maybe an epiphany awaits us beyond the sanctuary edges of our favorite foods.

And so, we've set this table with hopes that you'll contemplate exactly that. And perhaps be inspired to bring a dish of your own to our next gathering.

For now—*enjoy.*

Thimbleberries

T. Clear

On an uphill slog and a trail
that seems to go nowhere: thimbleberries
at their peak, dangling like rubies
in the forest's green shade.
Berries so delicate that, despite my care,
the two or three seconds
from branch to lips is enough
to dissolve their sweet wonder
into druplets, my fingers
sticky and stained.

Better to graze lips-first like a deer
without risk of bruising.
Quicker on the tongue that way.
Their not-quite boysenberry,
not-cranberry tang hints
of dusk, of sunlight diminishing,
bass notes that linger
long after this grey-haired poet
has groaned herself to standing,
continued on up the trail.

Instructions

—after Jeffrey Thomson's "The Tale of the Alphabet"

Niccolo Bechtler

"Language is a male discourse."

—Gloria Anzaldúa

Begin from a place of myth. After all,
this is where places come from.

Tell it clearly, starting with the basics:
who was there in that human world, what they said,

the stories told in their wake. When you use
metaphor, do it modernly, like a dial tone.

Write in paragraphs.

Foreshadow the conflict of your story
by introducing the presence of the gods,

the self-defeating nature of their gifts:
divine objects, all, that bring suffering.

Remind your reader of whose name you sing,
on whom, in perceiving, you enact violence—

name her here.
                    Then admit conflict,
in this case, the gift of the written word.

Its incapacity to represent, its beguiling
facsimile of the landscape, how it hammered

the spirit into the shape of the psyche
and left us further from heaven than when we started.

Now, remember the irony of what you are doing
and try to phrase it, somehow,

as if you are not in mourning.

My Imagined Drink of Possibility

Dana Stamps, II.

You're not going to believe this,
but I actually came
up with an idea for an invention, the first time
in my life, literally; and now,
I'm an inventor (my obituary will need to be rewritten,
reset in new stone). Probably,
my idea has been thought of before,
so I'm likely
to have egg on my face, but here it is:
an "endless cup"
of cold water. Endless, you say? Yes, there are devices
that can pull
moisture out of the atmosphere
and slowly make drinking water. Big,
clunky contraptions. Boats often have them, yachts
and such. So imagine

a thermos-sized gizmo that can (1) pull moisture
from the air itself,
and (2) do it fast enough
that a person sipping will never,
literally, never

run out; and (3) it keeps the water cold (or
hot?) so that the temperature of
the last swallow is as cold
as the first swallow (of course, the more advanced
models will replenish two-swallows
for every one-swallow
of the drinker, guaranteeing the "Endless Cup"

phenomenon). And, as I think of it,
in the arid places
where there is not enough safe drinking water,
this will be a God send.
Reporters from the *Wall Street*
Journal will ask: How does it feel to have solved
the world water
crisis? and our Chatterati, Inc., will ask: How does it feel
to have saved
capitalism itself? Hell,
I will have to pay expensive,
hoity-toity publicists
to come up with good answers to that *cash*tastrophe.
Should I get this idea
patented before The End of Daze?

And, one last thought, to put this idea
into clear,
potable perspective: maybe the water (or diet soda, tea,
coffee, moonshine, etc.) will eventually be,
by some-grand-

scientific-how, transmitted *through the air,*
and Perrier will
tah-dah (or even better in the French *viola*) appear
in your "Endless Cup®"
by Have-a-Drink-On-Me, Inc.
All for an itsy-bitsy fee.

This technology will be possible in the
future, but rejected as unclean, my Holy Grail "never
empty so it can be
washed," a conspiracy theory,
obviously.

Impulse Buying the Future

Yvette A. Schnoeker-Shorb

Succulent dreams, rich nightmares,
my neurons have developed
a taste for drama, as if this body
is someone else's, sweat-moist,
waking, more like sleepwalking
to nab a midnight morsel
beyond the dimly lit kitchen
on the way to the portal
of doom-scrolling, trolling
the world screen by screen.

Cat on my lap, dog by my feet,
they rest peacefully, cease
dwelling on any nonsense
from the day before. I should
be more zen like them, but then
how do they plan for a nation
collapsing? And yet night falls
into scarlet sunrise, my house-
plants sense the light, my lover
begins his daily affirmations

even as I confirm my fears.
Surely there is something here,
news or views. If I can just settle
on a sweet site to make things right.
Behind me, he wanders barefoot
in his dark blue robe, whispers
to the ferns and philodendrons,
talks to the peccary curled up
on our back deck, joyfully greets
a long-legged spider on the ceiling

while I keep searching the web
for reassurance. If I can just find
those tempting pages designed
to put my raging mind at ease,
entice it to release dopamine,
serotonin, oxytocin, anything
but adrenaline—it's all about
obsession, compulsion, control,
stress-driven consumption
of a future that doesn't exist.

Patriarchy-Made

Maryam A. Ghafoor

This hair on my knuckles
& all over—now, that's mine.
Not enough lasers in the world
to burn my thick & luscious follicles.
My stretch marks are growing.
Opposite of fake is this nose
right here in all its blackhead glory.
Which isn't to say I haven't
thought about it, the difference
between "elected" and
"for your survival." Hasn't
every "deviated septum"
had to snap back with a
leave my bone-bag alone
or else, a yes to the scalpel
so swift, even the swiftest
wing-beating swallow
couldn't bank it back
to its limestone roof
in time for the IV, nod to sleep,
and that jaundice-colored
antiseptic all over your face?

Patriarchy-Made

I remember the TV show
The Swan. The shape of those
rods under skin
suctioning so forcefully
her torso lifts off the table
while we become the very names
whale blubber oil surgeons extract
as if her/my/your body
an animal's & how violent
they all were, especially us
on the couch watching
imagining that knife
in our bellies
sing-praying please,
just let us
keep
alive-safe
this tissue
human
warm
& ours.

The Problem of Describing Color

—after Robert Haas

Celia Lawren

Not exactly blue, I say. *Closer to turquoise.*

We're crossing the maw of Viedma Glacier,
on Lake Cristina, arm's reach from a shimmering iceberg.
It's slow moving, as if hesitant to leave its mother.

Definitely blue-green, leaning toward green, you say.
Did you know the surface of an iceberg absorbs
all the reds and yellows, leaving blue behind?

You smile, pleased with your recall.

Yeah, I reply. *Angles of light are tricky. What you see and I see*
can be different even though we're standing close.

A woman in a red knit cap with a face like a roadmap
leans over and, in a raspy whisper, tells us,

Goethe said colors are the deeds and sufferings of light.

Ah! we say, turning back to the iceberg, the glacier.

*(for Simon Perchik)

Cal Freeman

*

Little star, estoile,
C-star describing
a vibrating string

in Hilbert space,
all-encompassing

Perchik title, shift-8,

asterisk, redactor of the names
of the forever innocent,

*

guide us to the note
that qualifies and complicates
the declarative assertion

*(for Simon Perchik)

that the world exists
and notate the putative merit
of the history of the

historical present
disembodied in the sentence,

Decades ago
I talk to Uncle Joe from Tulsa

*about McGwire's**
home run chase.

*

Bombardier of the immaculate assumptions
concerning the interrelatedness of strings

of anecdotes, divider of what
might otherwise bleed together,

*

do not cut the mill wheel
from its stream, but excise
the notion that narrative
must culminate in power
(god bless the go**amn*d
powerless),

*(for Simon Perchik)

that policy can be reduced
to slogan,
that the sloganeer is an agent
of ill intent.

*

Little star, estoile,
lone star I'm able

to draw by hand,
crude star of intersecting

lines, asterisk,
C-star, what is

the function of your staid
discretion while

mother*u**ers (holomorphs)
refract invective

and the analog
opens on the infinite?

After Thunder

Madronna Holden

After thunder chose you

you walked backwards
toward the sky

flailing your arms
in imagined water

twisting your tongue
on big man talk

roaring like thunder
showing the current
between us all.

Heyoka: this is why the people stand
to honor you:

To thank you for your hard ride—
with all the broken bones
this cost you.

To thank you
for the bucking-backward truth
in you that makes disease
lose its way.

To thank you for being
chosen by the thunder beings —
and not turning away.

There is always room for death between microwaved meals

Daniel Brennan

The slit of throat through the plastic
enough for a gasp enough

for me to breathe too. I never thought
grief would be simple but

I had not pictured this:
the familiar slam of a door, the chirp

of buttons as timing is selected,
the rumbling click as my meals

rotate around heat's heavy fist.
The world is so tired

of me, and I so tired of it;
at least we've learned to agree

on something. The breaths still come,
the *ding!* of the microwave

relentless as I sustain ritual which
becomes survival. The light from within

an unblinking eye; I've never
known how to handle a standoff, have I?

Still, I have to eat. I must do this
over and over again because I'm told

I must live by those who know better than me.
Steam rises from food; what God reveals himself

amidst this: an endlessly resurrected
carnage? When I open my mouth it is the howl

of clock counting down. Time, making
a morsel of me the same. That struggle into waking,

twisting in the heat, coming back
to life against the odds. The chime as task

comes to completion. When the food is ready I am
almost afraid to ask: *is this living?*

This is the Year

—after Martin Espada's "Imagine the Angels of Bread"

Dariana Guerrero

This is the year the tenants take over the tenements
revolutionizing the projects
with the momentum
of Taíno arrowheads
or the power of the raised fist

this is the year
we throw out   citizenship
as arbitrary stamps of a dream
fully realized draping ourselves
in the wrinkle of a creased bandera,
we crumple the threads of nationality
and border walls.

This is the year
fire hydrants are used as sprinklers
in the concrete playgrounds
of the hood, cooling the pavement
beneath youthful toes, soothing
the sweltering scorch of the sun.

This is the year
new life has nothing to fear
growing from the wombs
of women of color forced
into sterilization by governmental authorities
looking for black and brown servitude

this is the year mothers swaddle their infants
in intergenerational strength, the bondage of trauma
cleansed like a limpia performed in the back of Papi's bodega.

This is the year ICE is dismantled
and put on trial, greeted with the faces
of ghostly small children, Justice shivering
up the spines of the system as they look
into the eyes of DREAMERS.

This is the year we can't look away.
The turning of a neck is as dangerous a weapon
as white women's tears

this is the year doctors believe
the painful cries of the laboring Dominican
mother, the Haitian man with gout
the inner-city teen asking for birth control

this is the year we cancel microwave meals
everyone can afford to shop at Whole Foods
this is the year we eat: hearty, healthy, earthy

ancestral grains carried on the backs of the Atlantic
Slave trade.

If the revolution of the hood
began as a dream
of overthrowing whiteness,
then this is the year we summon
the rallying song of our fathers and mothers
Llegó, llegó, llegó la Rebelión y Joe Arroyo
dice *porque el alma, que el alma, que el alma*

el alma: a river of ancestral salty tears.

So may every bodycam reveal
the skeletons of this nation like
the rocky ash of a fallen city-state
excavating the tombs of our people,
laying their bodies   rest.

Real Food in an Imaginary Garden

Lee Rossi

—for EK

"Every thing has its own imagination,
sings its own song of praise," she said,
delving the orange cake's translation
of a recipe ported from her first wedding,
        handing each of us a slice
        flavored with cardamom and quince
        and honey steeped with rose.

Overhead the trails of seraphic
jumbos, and here a gray hairstreak trafficking
with lupine and yarrow, a setar's notes gliding
like ants hurrying in and out of hiding,
        reminding us to listen carefully
        for those who suffer despair,
        their voices whispering despair—

but for this moment we practice curiosity,
testing unfamiliar flavors with our mouths,
imagining ourselves in the ancient city
she came from, still in her youth,

filled with stories of battles,
ancient and modern, and walled gardens
where lovers dream of butterflies.

Here on Earth

T. Clear

At the side of the interstate, four lanes—
breakneck each way, no room
for hesitation—
a mother duck and ducklings
in a frantic scurry against a concrete barrier.
A blink in time
and already I'm well beyond them
at 60 miles per hour,
only headlights in the rear view.
Silly to think
there's someplace to pull over.
To do what, exactly?
I'm no Moses.

I want to believe they found
a break in the wall,
scuttled down and away
from what is not meant for anything
but hurtling steel.
That they found a wet-enough puddle
for their downy flotilla.

That their wings lifted them, finally,
from this hell.

entrañas

ire'ne lara silva

i do as my gods bid they do not command i do not obey but i listen to what my entrañas say and what are my entrañas but the godvoice that lives inside my body deeper than my flesh my gods are a flame my gods are the petals of a sunflower my gods are a translucence of skin

i heard the earth laughing heard its delight as it made the roads ripple made pipes burst snapped power lines made the tiny people scream in fright made the tiny people run i felt the drunken joy of the earth as it shook itself free and reclaimed its face reclaimed its abilty to gaze at the sky

they told me no one prays to the gods of hurricanes anymore no one prays to the gods of wind anymore that isn't what souls are for but everyone is afraid of change and i am terrified of things staying the same and the godvoice whispers *death is the only thing that never changes*

twenty-eight pomegranates

Nicholas Barnes

i dreamed i was a pomegranate tree as tall as a giraffe. my little neighbors made their humble home around my shady roots and trunk. i leaned down and gifted them a chinese takeout bag with a six pack and a note, putting the last of my stash up for adoption on their grassy doorstep. hi there, hope you're doing well, stay cool. i've had this hangover for about two months running. one day i had an epiphany that i don't need to feel sick every morning. my pride went scuttling, whimpering away. waking up from the dream, i was still incommunicado with the universe. oh, how these deaths and devastations weigh so heavily on our shoulders. all our highs and habits will crescendo someday and come to a head. with luck, before our lows conclude in the depths of a graveyard hole. although i am awake, my dreams don't feel that much like fiction. so with latex balloons, ruffled party streamers, and betty crocker candle smoke in the air, i think i finally know how persephone trees celebrate summer birthdays like mine. they pluck out as many pieces of themselves as they are years old, and give them out to the world in jubilation. it's a miracle when you keep getting second chances. when your pomegranates stop growing green. when that old childhood sweetness returns, it feels like god could maybe love you after all. perhaps i'll ask him if spiraling counts as forward motion. maybe messing up is better than giving up. and you know we must go on. pomegranates fall down and rot, but in time, the seeds will send them forth again.

Vibrant Display Is Used to Ward Off Predators

Roy Bentley

I'm 8 and have picked up (from television)
that the cuttlefish is dependent upon coloring,
natural selection contingent upon persisting
and passing on traits. That October, the news
seeds different visions of goodwill; Americans
and Russians agreeing, once more, to disagree—
if fighting for peace is like fucking for virginity,
as George Carlin will say it is later in the decade,
we have always been full of shit up to our eyeballs.
This morning, Walter Cronkite warns of the missiles
targeting at Florida or Washington, D.C. All the while,
at the United Nations, Khrushchev rhetorically courts
hyperbole, language all that a dictator has sometimes.
At least till one or the other super power blinks and
the world is cuttlefish doing whatever cuttlefish do,
and men or women are free to reinvent themselves
in the Buckeye State with a lack of blue-sky days,
where it really seems necessary to praise the light.
If not question how much scarcity is, well, cruel.
My dad used to say that Ohio isn't Kentucky. Like
that explained everything one lacked and the other
was filthy with. Like real starvation was possible,

given wages and layoffs and the promise of jobs
where there are gators now, in the 21st Century—
likely as a result of flushing live pet-store reptiles.
Imagine alligators surprising deer in the darkness,
chomping down on indigenous and expatriate alike.
If the Universe is home to an unending free fall, it's
also the Western with James Garner and the roomful
of TVs my father is repairing, workbenches stacked
with Zeniths RCAs Admirals, the occasional exotic
brand before transistors, flickerings of cathode ray
picture tubes the Mystery's most recent iteration.

imma stay in namaste—

Abbie Doll

is what i wanna say (& *do* say just about every day, 'cause today, mantras *matter.*) but look!
at me—just another judy jetson, another p(l)ainfully white woman worming her way (in)
wriggling away (from) the banality of it (all) while you, a plain-jane bird, a robin with rust
-y foliage, forage in the dawn's delicate downpour, while i watch from a window with white-
washed walls, stuck in these hip-high quotidian weeds, trying, trying, *trying* to tame my mind
's rubik's cube disorder with these impossible-to-pronounce "peace-bringing" poses that all end
in -sana, but you say, *sauna?* & i say, *sure, lauren, sure.* 'cause whatever, you're distracting me
from my muscle breathing, & it's *literally* all i have since my non-tax-deductible "donations" to
the american healthcare system were wallet-wasted, reducing me to this anxious mud-stuck bod
& frenzied mind, so bitch please: if you're not here to help, step off the mat & outta my way!

Gravity

Gerri Brightwell

Up the wire ladder you go, pulling yourself hand over hand, foot over foot, each movement elegant and precise because down below there's always someone whose attention wanders from the ridiculous clown, on his ridiculous bicycle, blowing his tiny ridiculous horn. That clown—he's someone you never took seriously, a man with a soft belly and two chins, and yet, he's the one she loves now?

She's down there somewhere in her sequined leotard and headdress of pink feathers, watching because when your act is over, it's her cue to come bursting into the ring on a white horse. You, though, you haul yourself on against the pull of the earth. The higher you climb the fainter the clown's tooting grows until there's nothing but your own laboured breathing. Overhead, a tiny platform you hoist yourself onto as the ringmaster's voice belts out. Now the white glare of the spotlight finds you and you arch your back and lift one arm high, like a damn bird doing a mating dance, when it's too late for that.

Moments later, a drum roll—a sound soft as distant rain—and you step out onto the wire. First you settle one foot, then sweep your other around in front of it, and here you are, suspended. Between you and the sawdust, there's nothing but a chasm of empty air, and how glorious it is to step across it, to bend and fling yourself in perfect tumbles that land you bouncing back on the wire. Up here, you are magical; up here, you are lighter than air. Oohs and aahs waft up from below, but what is the crowd to you? No, this performance is for her.

How time slips away, though. Already there's the final blast of your music, and you bow with your heart knocking against your ribs like a trapped bird because you feel the earth tugging at you once more. You've spent your life teasing it, evading it, but now you bend your knees and launch yourself, legs neatly together, arms spread, and if you had wings you'd be gliding, and if you were a hawk you'd see her face down below, wide-mouthed with horror. But you, you are only a man giving in to gravity at last, plummeting through the gasps of a crowd still waiting for the trick that will save you.

Anna No, Anna No

Joshua Zeitler

A bartender and a regular, we sit on a patio picnic table smoking cigarettes, the drone of a guitar playing "Free Bird" rattling the bench beneath our feet. The sun stabs through a busted picket in the fence, and the open sky—like a wet sheet, dipped—soaks crimson at its edges. Mottled purple blossoms peek from behind the foundation on her neck. She pulls a joint from her hoodie pocket. Smooths it tenderly. Pinches the crutch in her lips, sucks in, holds the butt to the twist until it flares. Flame there, then gone. Sweet smoke curls around our shoulders. Wordlessly, she points up, dragging our gazes over jagged white tracks criss-crossing the sky. Gathering their volumes, bearings. We fill our lungs in rank and hurried breaths. *Chemtrails.* she says at last. *Huh*, I say. Her red eyes glisten as if she's been crying. She's the wife of the open mic night's host—his third—not a performer, though she can be talked on occasion into singing the nonsense version of "Yellow Ledbetter." The misheard lyrics, delivered just off-key, never fail to rouse laughter from a packed and nervous crowd. But no one is here tonight. *See more and more of this in the lead-up to November*, she says. *Trying to keep patriots sick and complacent at home, out of the voting booths*. She shakes her head. *They don't like how Killary's polling. We'll show 'em.* We're getting down to the end of our smokes. The final notes of "Free Bird" stall in our shaking laces. No applause, only sudden silence. *Singing tonight?* I ask. She takes one last drag, nodding her whole body to an imaginary beat. She yowls: *On a ceiling, on a porch of glitter...*

If I lift my arm

I could touch her, that's how close

we are.

i thought i was a storyteller

ire'ne lara silva

—for Donna Barba Higuera

a collector of stories someone who listened to and loved and learned stories stories to tell others to tell myself thought i learned them by heart so that i'd never have to be without a story learned them so well i heard them in my own voice learned them so well i could carve my own stories out of them learned them so well i thought i could hear my new stories and the old stories keeping each other company

i've said it before everything is made of stories the sunlight is a story the sun tells the night is a story the stars tell the trees flowers grass are stories the earth tells every man woman child beast bird fish is a story life tells our bodies are stories time tells desire is a story skin tells skin mouth tells mouth heat tells heat love is a story told by the parts of us that never die

i thought i was a storyteller i always loved looking at faces that seemed delighted to listen loved it when people closed their eyes to listen more closely i loved the way stories felt when i carried them in my belly in my eyes with my arms and legs my flesh suddenly made strong and eternal the neverending wonder of discovering the stories i told as i wrote them

storytellers go on adventures to have new stories to tell to learn new things or to remember stories they forgot storytellers go on adventures because new places remind them how much they love all the old places storytellers go on adventures to be shaken out of their skins their comfort their solid beliefs and what i learned is that i don't just tell stories i eat them i breathe them

i drink them i pray them i sleep them and they eat me they breathe me they pray me into being what i learned is that a storyteller is a story and that stories should never be held captive you kill stories when they aren't free like trapped wolves they'll gnaw at their own legs to get free a story needs freedom a story needs air a story needs the road

a story needs to be able to move to fly to run a story needs to be able to change a story is a living thing a hungry thing a thirsty thing a wanting thing a story needs open sky hay necesidad de tierra libre aire libre una alma libre una lengua libre i have spent my entire life fighting to be free with hands like claws with teeth and blood

this last adventure reminded me beautiful prisons are still prisons and now i have a new story to tell how softer years can wear away at your vigilance how softer years can keep you from seeing the glint of steel how the story of life will find a way to tell you a story loud enough to make you listen and the story i am won't falter again a story must be free

belonging

Nicholas Barnes

Come summertime, i'd walk through grandma june's backyard to the tree line above indian creek. a place called happy camp, formerly murderer's bar. my home away from home. i could be a kid there. i remember buzzing with excitement at the edge of the chestnut grass. then the scramble down the steep canyon path to my favorite swimming hole. hours of splashing in the crystal current, wary of rattles and fangs. prospecting the fish highway for gold nuggets but settling for iron pyrite, crawdads, and trout parr. ambling along the silt streambed carrying a small boulder, imagining i was a cousteau or armstrong. skipping stones up and down my enchanted klamath tributary. jumping underwater to lose the horse flies and mosquitoes. one time, retiring for the night, i headed back up the bank and fell into a poison oak jungle. all i could do was wait for the weeping rash. red as the clay the noxious plant sprouted from. but despite the dangers, it was in those jade green pools where i felt i most belonged. always moving houses, i was grateful for this stationary paradise. it was good luck in bloom. it was seeing my grandparents. maybe a little fishing. smacking river rocks with a baseball bat. back then, i'd cry every time i embarked on or returned from a trip. i was a sentimental child, hungry for the meaning of home. so i tried to turn everywhere i went into one. even today, part of me is still in that living water and sweet smoky mountain air. i'd jump headlong into that thicket again just to spend one more summer in the siskiyous. getting sun drunk and nursing a nasty souvenir under the watchful gaze of loving eyes.

Silver Street

Jennifer Randall Hotz

Her sister's the one
who tells her that the house
they grew up in is for sale again,
a price-per-square-foot put on

the entryway
where they dragged newspapers
in long before the sun came up,
folded them in half, stuffed them
into rough canvas bags, headed out;

the front room
where Dad always tried to
center the Christmas tree,
sweated to secure it into the stand,
asked, *Is it straight?* (while it
careened from side-to-side),
cursed as he stood up
to find it crooked yet again;

the TV room
where Mom would sit

in her nightgown snacking on
wedges of raw cabbage
(certain that this time, this diet
would work) nursing one of seven kids,
her belly rounding as soon as
the most recent baby left diapers;

the dining room
where night after night
they told tales about
their days, laughed
and cried and argued;

where even way back then,
they all dreamed of leaving
this place—thought surely
they were meant
for so much more
than this.

A Man Shuffles Off His Porch

Ann Farley

and says:
Nice dog, nice dog.
Is German Shepherd?
I know this kind of dog.
My grandfather was fire chief in Vietnam
        and one day someone give him dog just like.
When my grandfather retire, he give dog to our family.
I was just boy.
Dog's name was Ne, N-E, like North East.
We love dog, we love Ne,
        but when we are rescued, when we go to get on ship
        to come to America, we cannot take dog with us.
They say no dogs, only people.
No dogs. Only people.
We have to leave dog.
Our neighbors tell us after we leave
        dog goes back to our house, lies on each of our beds.
Then dog leaves,
        goes out into fields to die.
I am just boy then,
        but I never get another dog.
I miss dog so much.

Never again, never again.
Seeing your dog, so handsome, makes me happy.
So smart, so loyal, this kind of dog.
Thank you for coming by.
What is his name?
Ella?
Ah. Nice dog, very nice. Beautiful.
Thank you.
You let me tell you about Ne.
Thank you.

Every Life Has a Purpose Shovel

Linda and Bob Blatz

"Every life has a purpose, and I've come to realize mine is to give everyone else a better one."

—Margot 2008

	You were my daughter in
every	sense of the word.
	We wish there had been more time to see how your
life	would unfold.
	Our world
has	changed in some important, irrevocable way. You showed
a	selflessness driven by what you felt was your
purpose	—caring for others—
and	your confidence, your sense of
I've	got this.
	I intended to raise you in a way that would allow you to
come	into your own,
to	think prior to acting, step back and
realize	rash moves are rarely effective.
	I was told your addiction was your business not
mine	What I did learn
is	gut instinct is sometimes the only thing you can count on.

<table>
<tr><td></td><td>Addiction was never a way out for you but a fight</td></tr>
<tr><td>to</td><td>stay alive. Maybe you'll</td></tr>
<tr><td>give</td><td>me the forgiveness I'm seeking. Leave me</td></tr>
<tr><td></td><td>with a memory that</td></tr>
<tr><td>everyone</td><td>who encountered you immediately liked you and</td></tr>
<tr><td></td><td>enjoyed your interpretation of the world.</td></tr>
<tr><td></td><td>All</td></tr>
<tr><td>else</td><td>is white noise. I wish I had been</td></tr>
<tr><td>a</td><td></td></tr>
<tr><td>better</td><td>listener,</td></tr>
<tr><td>one</td><td>who would provide for and protect you.</td></tr>
</table>

Beyond the Haze

Grace Whitmore

I only moved to Haze, California because I received no internship offers the summer after my junior year of college. I had applied to work at architecture firms, design start-ups, museums, journals, and countless other offices, and when none of them hired me I tried cafes, bars, and restaurants, and then I decided I'd just go home to Oregon for the summer. I had been searching plane tickets online before an art history lecture when Hope, who sat beside me, told me about the job in Haze. Hope, with warm eyes like paintings and long hair like curtains. Hope, whose laugh was like a goose's guffaw. She'd been describing her summer internship at a literary magazine when she mentioned her dad, a film executive, had an acquaintance who was hiring.

"You'd be living in a very small place," Hope told me. "I'd take the job myself, but I'm hopelessly cosmopolitan."

The town of Haze was a cluster of tired houses you could see in a single glance, and the house I lived in was one of the largest, and perhaps the tiredest also. I was employed by a retired English professor, Gwendolyn Pratt, and my job was to provide her companionship and conversation for the summer. Gwendolyn was a gentle woman who wore sweaters in hot weather and had likely once been beautiful. She was also losing her mind.

We spent most afternoons sitting on her back porch overlooking a gangly vegetable garden and trying to make conversation. "Johanna, what's your major in school?" she'd ask.

"Architecture," I'd reply.

"One of my dearest friends from back when I lived in LA was an architect," she'd say.

I cooked her meals, though this wasn't part of my job description, and I watched movies with her on a projector I'd set up in the living room. Anytime I asked her what she wanted to watch she said, "*Pride and Prejudice*!"

I had brought my copy of *Pride and Prejudice* along with a few other classics thinking they'd be good conversation starters. One morning a few weeks after my arrival I mentioned over coffee that I'd just finished reading the book a second time.

"That was the one with all the girls...who wanted to be...married," said Gwendolyn. I was surprised how thrilled I was to hear her make a correct statement.

"Charlotte Brontë wrote it," she said. "Or Emily?"

"Jane Austen," I replied.

"...was the eldest sister, the second to marry."

"Jane Austen wrote the book," I said. "Jane *Bennet* was the character who was second to marry." I tried to be chipper whenever I corrected Gwendolyn, but my corrections never failed to cloud her expression. She slumped in her chair like an admonished child and gazed into her empty coffee mug.

I had researched her the day I was hired. In a recorded lecture on *The Canterbury Tales* she moved across the stage with perfect alacrity, her every phrase clearly formed yet not at all rehearsed. Now, she looked up from her mug. "I'd like a coffee," she said. The instructions I was given at the beginning of the summer stated that Gwendolyn was allowed only one cup per day. I reminded her of this and asked if she'd like to go for a walk.

Gwendolyn's road was pale. A palm tree guarded the corner of her property. She shuffled. "How long have you lived here?" I asked.

"Well," said Gwendolyn. "A while."

It was only June and I had two months left in Haze before I returned to college. While other girls I knew worked tech internships in unfamiliar cities or taught English abroad, I was a glorified babysitter in a pin-prick town whose most pressing responsibility was to know when *Pride and Prejudice* was written, and who had done so, and to know this again and again. It was all the better because I wasn't much of a conversationalist, and I thought if Gwendolyn had all her faculties I would run out of things to say to her. In class I stayed silent and when I did speak my phrases interrupted each other while my mind remained eerily quiet.

We veered onto Main Street and passed the general store where I grocery shopped. The Pit Bull lounging in front raised his head and tapped his tail on the pavement. A restaurant advertised "Two Dollar Tacos."

"That place looks good," said Gwendolyn.

I smiled. "We'll have to try it sometime." We had been there the week before.

The rest of June I spent walking to the gas station near Gwendolyn's for cheap corn dogs, taking photographs of white-tooth gravestones in the cemetery at the edge of town, and trying to come up with the right text to send Hope to thank her for my summer job. Even in person I struggled to converse with her. She'd been steeped in the film industry from birth and had come to college with all the right references, all the right connections. She was a *writer*, and she didn't know this, but so was I, though I'd never completed a piece of work beyond essays required for school. For me, writing was a drumbeat echoing through my mind that I prayed would one day sound aloud. Then all the others would know how talented I was, and I'd lie back and look at the sky without fear, without speaking another word. Hope's fiction had been published in an LA based literary magazine. I paid for a subscription so I could read her piece again and again.

One afternoon Gwendolyn and I sat on the porch while I drafted a message for Hope in the notes app of my phone. The message needed to seem casual and offhand and this was difficult to cultivate.

"I've always found Elizabeth Bennet's character to be somewhat unbelievable," said Gwendolyn.

I looked up from my phone.

"I remember reading *Pride and Prejudice* as a child and thinking, 'she doesn't seem like the kind of girl who would gradually learn to admire a man. She seems like she would know right away if a man was one she could love.'"

Gwendolyn did not wait for my reply; she wobbled to the top of the stairs leading down to her garden. For a moment she stood poised, arms hanging like those of an ape, then she turned to me saying, "Jane Eyre was lucky she could see so clearly. Otherwise she and Mr. Rochester could have never been together." I leapt up to help her down the stairs and to the nearest garden box full of acorn squash.

"I would think they'd be ripe by now," said Gwendolyn.

"It's only July," I reminded her.

When we returned to the house, I offered to make sandwiches but she only asked for a second, forbidden coffee. I poured us each a cup.

The following day Haze yellowed with heat. Lying on my bedroom floor with a washcloth over my forehead and a fan running, I called my friend Ivy who was conducting biology research on campus.

"They never told me Gwendolyn had early-onset dementia," I said. "I thought I'd be her companion, but I'm more of a home health aid."

Ivy was sympathetic. "I bet you make more than I do at this research job," she said. "My stipend feels like hardly enough to cover groceries."

I didn't know how to explain how badly I craved a job like hers that would lead me to other, fancier, jobs. The kind I'd feel proud mentioning to a professor. The kind Hope had. Ivy *was* correct though—I made decent money working for Gwendolyn, and the money piled up in my account without a way to spend it because there were no restaurants or bars in Haze. A small place.

"Do you ever see Hope around campus?" I asked. "I heard she's living in student housing."

"From afar," said Ivy. "I love how she dresses. Sometimes when I'm lying in my dorm I can hear her laughing down on the street."

Gwendolyn tapped my door. "The acorn squash," she said. "They'll need more water in this heat."

"I watered them this morning," I called.

Gwendolyn did not reply.

I found her hovering at the top of the porch stairs playing her fingers across the railing. I rushed to help her down. In the heat, the top layer of soil surrounding the acorn squash had lightened. I turned on the hose and mist blurred the plants and darkened the soil and rainbows curved and danced. Gwendolyn was entranced. "Do you want to hold the hose?" I asked. She looked at me like this was the kindest offer she'd ever received. When I placed the hose in her hands the water seemed to falter.

There were other plants in the garden—zucchini and broccoli, green beans and red peppers—but Gwendolyn favored the acorn squash, last to ripen.

"Did you enjoy your career as an English professor?" I asked.

"It's a wonderful vocation," said Gwendolyn. "I think my one true talent is reading novels. I had to train myself to write and speak well. Those skills didn't come so naturally."

"Were you always so dedicated? Or was there a time when you yearned to work but had no idea what you were supposed to be working on?"

Gwendolyn tugged the hose toward the final acorn squash. "I feel that way now," she said. "But then I think of all the lecture series I've spoken in and all the books I've written, and I remind myself I'll never be forgotten."

"You won't," I said. "I'll never forget you."

The squash leaves were heavy with gems. "I love my work," said Gwendolyn. "I only wish I had more time to garden."

Una foto con la cara de mi padre trozada por una tijera.

(original poem from Piélago / Pelagic Zone, Spanish language, Mexico)

Irma Torregrosa

Una foto con la cara de mi padre trozada por una tijera. Había otra quemada por una de las esquinas. De mi padre quedaba lo que hay después de un vaso roto en la cocina. Astillada con su nombre, mi madre desangró sus mejores años en una tarde, mirando hacia la única ventana que había en nuestra casa.

Antes de irse, mi padre puso sus ojos en mis cuencas y la boca torcida de cuando se enoja.

: eres como él.

Fui, entonces, luz acurrucada en los brazos de mi madre. Después, como él, los restos de un vaso roto que ella buscaba unir todas las noches, inútilmente.

Una foto con la cara de mi padre trozada por una tijera.

Los buenos tiempos quebrados por el llanto de una niña que grita porque sueña que se ahoga. Mi madre hurgaba dentro de mis ojos, buscándolo. Calmaba mi llanto y cerraba los ojos mientras se imaginaba desnuda nadando en las cascadas chiapanecas, a donde dice que fueron cuando se casaron.

A donde dice que fueron cuando eran felices,

antes de mí.

In one photo, my father's face has been snipped to ribbons by scissors.

(translated poem, English language)

Allison A. deFreese (translator)

In one photo, my father's face has been snipped to ribbons by scissors. In another, a corner has been burned. What remained of my dad were the fragments from a broken glass in the kitchen. Shattered by his name, my mother bled out the best years of her life in a single afternoon as she gazed out our only window.

Before he went away, my dad placed his eyes in my sockets and left me his twisted mouth when he gets angry.

: you're just like him.

At the time I was a streak of light curled up in my mother's arms. Later, like him, I became the shards of a broken glass she tried in vain to reassemble every night.

In one photo, my father's face has been snipped to ribbons by scissors.

The good times were smashed to glass by the cries of a little girl who screams when she dreams she is drowning. My mother rummaged around in my eyes, trying to find him. She calmed my sobs and closed her eyes as she imagined herself swimming naked at the waterfalls in Chiapas where she says she and my dad went when they were newly-weds.

Where she says they went when they were happy

and before I was born.

Bowls of My Father's Anger

Scott T. Hutchison

As God is my skeptical witness—I've read the whole Bible, and I've had it sorely explained to me. I have a mean knuckle-rub of understanding on many a holy quote, like those regarding reaping and sowing, and Jesus knows I've slurped enough soup from the Lord's final Bowls of Wrath. Still, there's powerful Proverbs warning how "hatred stirs up strife," even though there's another passage telling us that there's six things the Lord himself *hates*, and "seven that are an abomination to him." While pinning down where the Good Book lands on uncontrolled detestation—a puzzlement I've duly rassled with—me and the Lord can probably agree that the abomination has something to do with paternity.

Gasp Cave Baptist Sunday School and Vacation Bible School accomplished two of three salvation tasks on my behalf, missing only on the Big Dunk. Church, prayer, and concepts of the Father function differently for me than for most people, because worship and respect strike me as awfully funny things. I've dressed myself every Sabbath and walked the half mile to Church, rain or shine—every week and summer—fulfilling a promise I made to my sweet mama on her deathbed. I've given it all a charitable listen. Church teachers tell me that Psalms and Lamentations and the Samuels are the dearest, most moving of all the Books, though John and Matthew have their devout enthusiasts. Most of the kids I know favor the earthy stories found in

Genesis. Me—still undunked at age twelve and about to move into the Young Men classes—I accept the Word on different terms from the rest—I'm a Revelations Man.

My church accepts gospel in a "damnation, boy—every word is true" kind of way, hoping I'll accept enlightenment and get myself baptized. Which is complicated when we're examining prophesy rather than straight-up stories on snakes and temptations and lion dens. I can't talk about the *future* of Christ and his Big Daddy finally cleaning house and creating Heaven On Earth, because I've been there, done that. Bowls of Wrath pouring over the wicked and temporary physical world? *My* daddy—as sinful a specimen of humanity as any who've ever crawled, a demon scourge who would slap an Angel for a nickel—he full-bowl taught me all about the End Times.

I still have visions of Daddy hurling infuriated bowls, along with every other piece of china in the kitchen. Schooled as I am in the Signs, this first indication of Heavenly plague became plain when Daddy got himself visited upon with some kind of nasty pecker disease. I don't know rightly if there was scabs or disfigurement or some other beastly symptom, but he got eruption-angry during every voiding for a two-week span of urination agony. I tried not to imagine what he was going through when he insisted I should picture God throwing toothpicks and lightning bolts with cursed accuracy, dispassionate weapons spearing his sausage whenever he had to piss. He gritted teeth talking about his thick odd-colored discharge, spat out detailed reports of penile misfires and bowel movements, all of them sore and distressed and dire. Daddy'd have his evening drinks and try to hold back his water, but sooner or later the Bowl called his name. He'd walk bow-legged into the bathroom; I'd hear him burn his vocal chords in a hacksaw-scream, and when he finally reappeared, leaning and panting in the doorway, his brow and pits gushed like an opened fire hydrant. A week and a half in, he skittled outside to the toolshed after an episode, returned with a sledgehammer, and he punished porcelain for bearing false and comical witness to his pain. All that accomplished: we started using the third tree off back of the house for our business, normal or otherwise. Daddy finally found peace through doctor-pills.

I never laughed outright at the man—that would have been the End of me. But the two of us regularly caught our dinner by pier fishing on the weekends, casting lines out over the ocean in the company of a mirthless assortment of crusty cigarette-thin men. Every last one of them sipped from a two-quart thermos of questionable hydration. One bright morning Daddy's own green-skinned vessel had mysteriously become empty before nine AM. Me and some of the sun-brittle anglers listened to him disturb the morning with his curses, watched him rebaiting his hook—a 9/0 J-hook he hoped might pull a whale or a striper. He completely missed the shrimp he aimed for with the barb, but succeeded in punching high carbon steel into one end of his thumb and out the other. Then the fool began to full vent his wounded spirit, which gave me a sense that we were into Bowl II. No one had nippers capable of cutting it off at the barb to pull it cleanly back through. Daddy was splashing cut bait with his own blood, and then—though it had been a loyal friend for many a year—he hurled his empty Stanley Classic Vacuum Bottle, cup and all, out into the depths and turbulence, painted in scarlet handprint. Meanwhile, a fair amount of Daddy leaked out and down through the weathered boards of the pier. Though they remained mum, I watched the crow's feet crinkle with understanding at the corners of a lot of fishy eyes. I followed suit, keeping my giggles to myself. Looking out over the Atlantic, I pulled my line up when I saw dorsal fins cruising to taste injured changes in the water.

My Daddy achieved near-terminal velocity with throwing things after an even bloodier fiasco. It was end-of-summer, and we'd trespassed to a fine swimming hole in a crook of the local river, trying to get clear of second-cutting hay dust after scoring cash for tossing a farmer's bales. Daddy stripped down to grubby-grey undies and launched himself into a calm clear pool while I fiddled with untying my shoestrings. Unbeknownst to us, some a-hole—learned later it was one of Daddy's drinking buddies—had illegally dumped the bucket remnants of a field slaughter off the nearby bridge. Daddy, idly floating, called me every name of slow while cooling his noodle—he was happy as a turtle tongue, and ignored my speechless pointing aimed upstream—I froze when I caught sight of the atrocity drifting his way. His back was turned to Bowl III. Daddy's mirth globbed in his throat as the butcher water caught and slurped him. Primal cuts washed over and clung to the man, and he began slapping at the flotilla of risk materials that commenced henna-painting his whole body—bovine spinal cord, brain, and what I thought might be cow tonsils. He spit and splashed and took the Lord's name in vain and hurled away nearly the entire bed of river rocks. This incident proved to be a Bowl two-fer: Daddy cleared himself of the stream, bird-fluttered a dust-bath once he made shore, bubbled a pint of Old Crow in one pull and chucked the bottle into that red river of chuck—then he passed out, right there on the bank in full sun. Daddy cooked up like choice cuts on a barbeque, turning redder than his two-minutes-before red. In pure spite, once he woke up, he threw my sneakers in the trash after he'd baby-waddled his way home.

I own responsibility for Daddy finding his final Bowl of Darkness. Since I was maybe five- years-old, Daddy's made me help him with various stills he conceals on slopes and runs on the sly. Besides fire-stoking, getting rid of the first-run foreshots is one of my jobs. I'm supposed to take them a ways off and pour them down any hornet holes I can find. But I was angry about those shoes he'd thrown away in anger—with my own money I'd finally escaped the cheapy $12 Wal-Mart brands, purchasing my first-ever pair of Chuck Taylor's. Though the foreshots smelled like Zep hand-degreaser, I squeezed orange pulp into that first Ball jar of moonshine, masking the heady methanol. I left the jar out where he might grab it—meaning within arm's length of lazy. Good figuring. Daddy needed quenching, fingers grabbed the jet-fuel jar, and he threw it back. I rode out all his magnified evils that night, knowing what was to come. Next morning he got to tossing breakfast, then the world his eyeballs normally registered turned black. I'd scored another spare, another Bowling two-fer: Daddy blindly reached for copper and coil, grabbing and hurling every pot and jug and onion head he could grab hold of, waging war against the sinner he held responsible for his demise. He hurled every piece of contraption in the directions he suspected I was hiding. I watched the entire affair from a comfy branch, high in a beech tree. Doctors saved his ass with sodium bicarbonate, but even though he lived, his view of the world remained vague and distorted.

Six Bowls in, the Final Judgement came down on my Daddy in a fury, crushing him to smithereens. Like usual, he had the both of us catching fast, under-the-table cash, working out at Belletetes Bug Farm. They specialize in food sourcing for pet shops, meeting the needs of clientele partial to reptiles and amphibians. The Farm was working toward future plans for human consumption of natural protein, but I'd look at the zillions of compound eyes and antennas in the farm's aquariums, thinking *no thank you*. Belletetes also works with places selling to fishermen, offering live locusts for bait in addition to the usual fare of worms and crayfish. Me and Daddy were moving fish tanks used for incubating and raising the brood, carrying them from an old shed with running electricity to a new temperature-controlled barn. I could handle the ten and twenty-nine gallon containers of grasshoppers, while Daddy got all manly about the job, shouldering forty and fifty gallon tanks.

We were in mid-transit of bugs when a mighty rumbling started, a reverberation like powerful running horses thundering our way, ready to run us down. Sound arrived before sensation—and then an actual earthquake struck, shaking footing and teeth fillings to the root. Bad timing, some would say—yet another indiscriminate natural disaster. Seemed a bit more selective to me. I dropped the aquarium I was carrying, put my arms out to the sides and surfed out the tremor, watching as my Daddy tilted over sideways. He sensed the dangerous predicament on the instant, and tried hurling the tank a broad-sea measure away—but because his whole world had turned slant on him he actually tossed it straight up in the air. In that moment we caught each other's eye—and he threw it all at me, all the crazed turbulence and rage he carried in his heart, all the transgressions gone astray in his immortal soul. Recognizing what was near, I emptied out, throwing everything I'd ever been ladled right back at him in a seamless curve. Daddy looked like he was about to mid-air give me the bird, but that's when Wrath came breaking down, concussive shatters driving deep with two-fold plague: glass shards plunged into him like cave-buster bombs, ridden by thousands of green and brown big-legged pilots. Even when the earthquake stopped, the countless slices in his skin continued shivering like royal bug jelly—something the assemblage of herbivores decided to give a try.

I hope my mother watched from above and is happy with how the Finale worked out. And though I've never been formally baptized,

I sure as hell believe in God—so Mama needs to be content and settle her wings when it comes to how my faith has been revealed. Going forward, I trust in this simple truth: God don't play when he's handing out trial or tribulation or punishment. And that last Book of the Bible? All in all, it promises freedom, an end of Hell and the arrival of Heaven on Earth. Me and Daddy, we got what was coming.

Weltschmerz

Roy Bentley

It's Good Friday. We listen to the podcasters preach.
One wants to be credited with forecasting the decease
of what we let pass for democracy in the United States.
My wife Gloria earned an award in German in college.
She says *schadenfreude* means to feel pleasure or joy
at another's pain. She asks me to try and pronounce it,
and guffaws, loudly, like we're young and stupid again.
Once, she and I were walking in the Wisconsin marshes.
Some time passed, skies darkened, and we stood below
the Northern Lights. In houses, barking dogs contested
a coyote architecting a howl. Who would've believed
that a heart can break and then, completely unhealed,
break once more? The podcaster tosses out the word
for the world's hurt: *weltschmerz*. My pronunciation
occasions talk of forgiveness. Think: anguish but
continual. Add the Cross and Savior if it helps.

Ode to Line Cooks

Sara Burge

Burtis

Curly-haired lord of the Shoney's line,
son-of-a-bitch spurting nastiness through the pass—
my first braying ass of a line cook at my first gig
who tormented me every time
I wasn't right there to grab food.
I always looked down and said nothing
until the day I didn't.

Sunny

Pizza Hut Sundays meant Bible Belt Warriors
who'd given our tips to the collection plate.
Sunny had a joke about *getting on your knees for Jesus.*
Sunny was always first to offer
to spit in their food.

Brian

Fast food was easier,
but once I found fine dining's rhythm

and shirts that showed the perfect amount of tit,
tips grew fat, so juicy they covered the dresser
in my studio apartment with its chicken wallpaper.
The neighbor's door slamming me awake
was the perfect excuse to roll over and tell Brian,
I've got a double. Time for you to go

Juan

had a crush on me, but I had a boyfriend.
I wasn't into Juan then, but I am now.

Will

Downtown lizard always talking up his pierced dick,
though I did laugh that time he stood silent by the walk-in,
a slab of salami hanging out the front of his pants.
At an after-after party, he hollered
        Girls say riding my dick is like riding a shotgun!
then puked all over the couch.

Nate

All the waitresses hated Nate, who got off on making them cry.
I vowed he'd never make me cry.
After calling me the most worthless waitress he'd ever screamed at
        because my salads sat in the window too long
        I gave out too much bread not enough bread
        Bitch, why no FIFO?

I told him a customer said his alfredo was shit
so he screamed one last time, said, *Good, you didn't cry,*
then lowered his eyes,
offered me his Italian sausage.

Val

That summer after I got my fancy graduate degree
but couldn't get a job, I crawled back to where I swore
I'd never crawl again, slinging heaps of spaghetti
and praying for tips. I sweated garlic.
That summer, Val started slipping me trays of lasagna
saying she'd screwed up again. That summer
in the cheap rental stuffed with fleas, sweating
in the restaurant's bad AC, I acted like I didn't need
free food, but would do her a favor and cradle it home.
That summer, lasagna for lunch and dinner. Lasagna
for breakfast. Lasagna. Lasagna. Lasagna.

Kevin

knocked me up.
Line cooks and waitresses and bartenders
at our wedding. Our blond baby, too.

Makes a chile relleno
I'd almost trade that kid for.

~~~~~
~~~~~

Kevin, remember the guy we had over a few times
when our baby was still a baby?
He worked with you in the kitchen?
Helped us set up our computer?
Funny. Gentle.
OD'd. I found a picture of him
sitting on our couch.
Why can't I remember his name?

Hal

Scott T. Starbuck

It began with gift
of steelhead heart
to great blue heron

as he stood
10 feet away
until I left.

By third heart
he was 2 feet away
gobbling.

After that,
as I approached
deep river canyon,

Hal leapt
from high pine
to stand beside me,

our heads swiveling
in unison
as my bobber drifted

and plunged
with bright flash
of a fish.

"What's that?"
asked Derrick the logger,
amazed.

"This is Hal.
He fishes with me
each time."

"Most unusual,"
replied Derrick,
and it was.

Listening to Beethoven (with Cochlear Implants)

Suzy Harris

"There are many dissonances in the ideal world of tones.
Why, then, should it not be so in the real world?"
—from the copyist Ferd. Wolanck to Beethoven, January 1825

The winter he composes the first of his last Quartets,
Number 12, Beethoven is *very weak, vomiting,* needs
a *strengthening medicine.* Already deaf seven years—

even to music. *Tell the tailor to fetch the cloth*
for a pair of trousers, Beethoven says in a letter
to his nephew who was something like a son to him.

Bring anything in the shape of a newspaper, he writes.
Beethoven is unhappy with this nephew, with his *unbrotherly*
brother, with his copyists. Who can he trust?

Not even the cook. Two hundred years later, I listen
to this Quartet in a hall with a hundred others.
The man on my left reads the sheet music on his phone

as he listens, each note an exquisite bead he fingers,
music his elixir. Me? I am befuddled, my brain *bescribbled,*
some parts sounding so muddled, so dissonant.

Am I as confused as those first audiences? Do I hear
what that copyist heard? Beethoven was offended,
called him a *conceited ass of a fellow.* But maybe there's

some truth to it? *A failure,* Beethoven reported to his nephew.
And yet, later performances met *with the greatest applause.*
I hear that too. I hear those dancing melodies, entranced.

Note: *Italics* are from letters Beethoven wrote in early 1825, when Quartet No. 12 was composed/first performed. *Beethoven's Letters,* Selected & Edited by A. Eaglefield-Hull, Translated with Preface by J. S. Shedlock, B.A. (1926).

Listening to *Blood on the Tracks* at 71, I Decide the United States Needs to Acknowledge the Magic of Being and Be One Person

Roy Bentley

—for Al Maginnes

I first listened to *Blood on the Tracks* at Sherry Dixon's house. Her parents weren't home. We were alone together the first time. And it was as if This, All This made sense. Registered. Being alive. Like one's death and the pleasure and pain of just-existing counted the way a song can count, functioning mystically almost. And so, I'm remembering the first time Dylan sang *I can make it through, you can make it too* and I felt a coursing of confidence. A pride.

If not pride, then an epiphany. An OMG, regardless. I was sure I wouldn't be 21 forever, but I was going to remember it, by God. I'd remember the way Sherry unwrapped the record then put it on and let it register like years of practicing a skill and getting it right can register, sending shivers up the spine. So what's it like to be in the world? It's like hearing a remarkable record and feeling lucky. It's like falling in love with everything around you all over again.

Out in the Open

—*Guernica*, Reina Sofía National Art Museum, Madrid

Linda Jo Reinhard

In black, white, and gray
not a drop of red
Picasso renders eight figures

There is no need for blood
The broken sword, the screaming
tongues, the terrified horse, show all that is needed

After you see it no curtain can cover
the fallen man, the bellowing bull,
the stricken woman, the dead child

Valley Poltergeist in the Summer Months

Mazie McNamara

Two girls criss-cross on the outside brick
eating dark cherries. Poking the pits
into empty flower pot dirt. The neighbor's
over-eager Scottish terrier. Wet curtained towels
over barn red shoulders. I am sorry
for what I will do to you. Brown palms
and feet bottoms. Phone call. Phone call.
Staring at a clump of marbled dirt and crumbs
in the crack of a minivan. Thinking you'll remember
that instance forever. Parachute dome
on the mowed school grass.
Rock beach at the McKenzie River
with peanut butter and honey sandwiches.
Rock beach at the McKenzie River
alone hurling noise against the current
dunkplosh dunkplosh. Be generous
with the honey. You remember forever.
One girl yanks fistfuls of grass
piles it in the pool of her skirt.
The other smears cherry guts in circles
on her cheeks. I will come back again
soon I promise

The Tree

E. Laura Golberg

I watch the canopy from my bed,
green leaves in summer,
thin empty branches
when the weather is cold.

In June, a note from the city:
"We will remove this tree
in winter, due to its decay
and failing health."

A luminous red dot
has been sprayed on its bark
and paint has dripped on a weed:
glowing blood.

I must spend months
preparing for its loss.
How to imagine
what I will see out the window

when the tree has been cut.
There will be no going back

to compare the empty block of sky
to the shimmering leaves.

I could take a picture
from the bedroom window,
when the sky looks like
a Corot painting, but neither

he nor I can capture the breeze
riffling through the leaves,
the sun making shadows whirl.

the unrelenting everything

Abbie Doll

'twas a summer of feeling— / out of s(h)orts / feelin' sweaty / beggin'
for shade an' breeze an' /
feelin' chilly an' woozy an' / strugglin' with stayin' hydrated an' / chasin'
citrus as if it meant
somethin' / grapefruit this an' tangelo that / lemon sorbet an' key lime
pie / a summer of never
knowin' / much of anything / an' never ever / sittin' still

everyone was buzzin' 'round / pursuin' the season like / it was somethin'
to bottle / -rocket fire /
-flies and fire / -works, tongues hangin' / out—either pantin' or lickin'
/ the ridged shafts of
soggy waffle cones / that sweet race of a treat / doomed to ***drip*** / ***drip***
/ ***drip*** / same as your slick
skin / in those skyscraper-high temps / reachin' a hundred mo(i)st days
/ humidity wreakin'
havoc on your hair / -do an' even your local meteorologist is sayin' /
one look in the mirror will
tell ya

but in the midst of such summery things… / death crept in / -to our
most innocent season /
—*unforecasted* / like crabgrass encroachin' / smackdab in the middle
of yo' daddy's lawn /
leavin' us wonderin' / whatever happened to / that carefree guarantee /
? / tragedy used to be / a
neighbor you only ever saw / f r o m a f a r / both of you wavin' down
the street / sportin' your
new mechanical grins / playin' the part of two suburban ro(b)ots

an' now / there's this sweaty intimacy / as we occupy ourselves / strivin'
to keep the plants alive
/ stressin' ourselves questionin' / why caretakin' *never* comes easy / at
least not in this / summer
/ of drama   -tic // *f a d e* // that newborn, spring green l[aw]ng gone
/ browned by the harsh
sun of a solstice come an' gone / —just a flash in the pan / those endless
summer days / passin'
like a clump of clouds / with a subtle drift, an' yet determined / -ly, that
constant a.c. / hum
dominatin' the background / too hot for birdsong / too hot for windows
/ (accordin' to *you-know-*
who) / too hot for arguin' / too hot for dyin', too

and yet… / here we are / sweatin' in black / studyin' the ground / even
though it's way too hot
for standin' 'round / even the ghosts among us / are slippin' outta their
sheets / howlin' into the

spinnin' blades of your big box fan / seein' what sounds their mouths
might make / we *loved*
doin' that as kids / —remember / ? / had us a pocket of fun in an ocean
of boredom / but come to
think of it… / we sure as hell weren't hauntin' anyone / *so lay off, willya?*

Letters to Maha

Jessica Lawrence

Dear Maha,

So I saw Lucas Bell at Tyler Devlin's wedding last week and, well, the cat's out of the bag: I know you're pissed off about that letter I sent you last year, which I guess explains why I never heard back from you. You know, I had my reasons for writing it, which you already know.

Cross out "which you already know." Repetitive. First sentence is awkward as well. Forget explaining how you know. Lucas, that creep. Who tells somebody something like that, anyway?

Hi Maha,

Look, I'm sorry I wrote that letter. I'm sorry I wrote about a joke your dad once told, I'm sorry I mentioned anything at all. I see how it was in poor taste, and maybe I offended you culturally as well. Maybe Muslims don't believe in talking about the dead, or in remembering jokes their dead loved ones told.

Don't go there with the cultural stuff, just because everyone's hysterical about such things nowadays. Maybe it was culturally insensitive, but you were also best friends—beyond all that. Sentences still awkward.

Maha,

How's it going? How are things? The job at the bank? Fiancé? I do hope arrangements for the wedding are going smoothly.
Did she say she was engaged the last time you were in touch? Or just dating someone? Best not to mention it.

Dear Maha,

I've been meaning to write this note for a while, as it's been weighing on my mind. The thing is, I'm really sorry I sent you that letter when I found out your dad had died. *Passed away*? It was insensitive—I do see that now. It's just that I remember him so fondly from our expat days together overseas, and had gone through the same thing myself a few years earlier. Personally, I liked it when people reached out and recalled happy memories of my dad. *"I'll never forget how he would practice his violin every morning at dawn, in the bathroom for the acoustic effect." "I'll always remember his tie slung over one shoulder as he flipped pancakes so as to avoid the batter bowl." (He always wore a tie to work.)* Especially people we grew up with on the compound in Saudi, whom I hadn't seen for years now that we've all moved on from there. No one remembered any jokes my dad told, but he was a quiet man, as you know. Come to think of it, he didn't tell many jokes at all, although he did have a terrific sense of humor. Like your dad. That's why I mentioned the joke.
Far too much explaining. And don't talk about your dad. This isn't about you.

Dear Maha,

Here's the thing. We ran into Lucas Bell at the Devlin wedding last week, and he told me that the letter I sent you last year about your dad passing away had hurt you deeply. That's all he said—all he knew. And Maha, now it's weighing on me so heavily. I think it was because I mentioned a joke in a tragic context, but I'm not sure, and just thought I'd check. Could you let me know, when you have a moment? Oh, and if it was the joke, please allow me to extend my most heartfelt apologies.

What is this, a memo?

Hi Maha,

I know you've lived in Canada for a while, but really, no sense of humor anymore?

Not fair. You don't know anything about Canadians, or their senses of humor—you're just being rude about them because you've heard other people be rude about them. Why do people make fun of Canadians, anyway?

Dearest Maha,

Ummmm...

Hey Maha,

Come on, it was a great joke. A classic joke—the one about the Foreign Legion captain who has sex with a camel not understanding it was there to take the men at the desert outpost with "natural sexual urges" into town to find women. I can see your dad telling it now—those tufts of orange hair above his ears glowing in the light of the living room lamp. Hear him too—his thick Arabic accent. Aren't you pleased I remember these things?

Clearly, she isn't. Do you really want to ladle lemon juice over the wound by supplying a visual aid this time? Idiot.

Hi there,

Maha, I feel wretched. My life has been the pits since that creep Lucas Bell sat across from us at Tyler's wedding and told me the letter I sent last year had hurt you. I've always hated that guy. Remember how he used to make fun of me because my dad was a gynecologist? Remember how he said the word "vagina?" VaCHINEa. What a jerk. There was nothing for it after that but to go straight to the bar and order a large Chardonnay, which I downed within minutes. *Maybe leave this out. Remember, your friendship with Maha pretty much ended when you started drinking and she didn't.* Well, I know you were never one for the Chardonnay. Not that I was either; back then I didn't even know what Chardonnay was. It was all illegal homemade liquor in Saudi, and not very well made, at that. Remember how we mixed it with pear juice from the commissary and drank it in paper cups up at the golf course until we vomited? I know you didn't drink, really, but there was that *one* night. You drank more of the pear concoction than any of us and we had to wheel you home in my dad's wheelbarrow. My dead dad's wheelbarrow. Dad. Dead.

Yes, he died. My dad didn't pass away, Maha. He's dead.

Maha,

I know now that your dad—himself a military man—was telling us that joke to poke fun at the Foreign Legion and the idiocy of the West trying to survive its own brutal imperialism, but I think the moment was particularly memorable because sex was something we had only recently started learning about in school (and, to varying extents, from our families and friends). Remember you told me what a wet dream was, that time we were at the beach? We were eating vanilla ice cream cones and they were melting, sticky and cold, over our fingers.

The heat was throbbing. I knew about most things by then but hadn't heard of that one before. You said you'd seen your parents' sheets one morning and thought your dad had had one (your mom was away visiting her sister, so it couldn't have been sex). You'll note that I didn't write about your dad's wet dream in my original letter. I think the joke was in slightly better taste than that, don't you?

Ha.

Maha,

Who told you? Did your mom call? Or your sister? Or a doctor at the hospital, your mother perhaps too inconsolable to pick up the phone? What did the day look like, after that? It was the middle of August I believe. Was it the morning, the afternoon, the middle of the night? I imagine it being the middle of the afternoon. A warm, blue day in Vancouver. You were at the bank, maybe. These things never really happen in the middle of the night, do they?

No one needed to tell me. I was there. He spent seven hours and sixteen minutes on his last day heaving into a surgical mask. The doctor—a steely man from Aberdeen—told us my dad was aspirating due to an embolism, after being bedridden for months by the neurological disease that damaged his brain, and then killed him.

Remember the time we made my dad stop outside the U.S. Consulate on the fourth of July, on the way to get *shish tawooks* in Khobar? We wanted to see it because everyone in our class went there on the fourth to eat real hotdogs. Not that you ate pork, and I don't think I'd ever had it in my life. There were rumors of real beer too, though we weren't interested in that—yet. We weren't even drinking the homemade liquor—yet. We sat outside the iron gates and watched Marissa Hagan and her parents walk right in. What a strange feeling, to want to storm that fortress surrounded by palms nodding in the wind. One ugly building represented a world to us—closed to you as a Jordanian Canadian, closed to me with British parents. It was a small moment, but it had a shape and a weight.

Then, on that same outing, a mutawa in Khobar hassled us because your abaya wasn't long enough to fully cover your legs, even though you had slacks underneath—he swatted at your ankles with his cane. You cried all the way home and said that we were outsiders who didn't belong anywhere—not with the Americans at the consulate, nor with the Saudis in Khobar. Even though you spoke Arabic, you felt that way too.

I wonder how your mother took the news. I was always a little afraid of her, to tell the truth. I would have had a harder time remembering a tender moment, were she the one to have died. You once told me that your mother performed routine checks to make sure you were still a virgin. At the time, I remember thinking this was entirely appropriate, even edifying, and secretly wishing my mother would do the same. How honorable it seemed, next to the antiseptic things my father did at work.

Now I think you made that up. She can't have been *that* worried. She can't really have put a finger up there to see what she would find. That would be considered a perversion nowadays. Back then, too. *Leave out the part about her mother fingering her. The rest is getting there.*

Maha,

Come to think of all this stuff, I've now remembered something else that happened after we'd grown apart. I'd started hanging out with the Devlins and all of those kids, started going up to the golf course regularly, and you'd written me off as a drunk and a slut. Which maybe I was. But there was that one summer we were all home—you from Canada—and you called me out of nowhere. Remember that? You needed my help. No, you needed my *dad's* help. You'd been living with your first boyfriend—some jerk from Italy who was in Vancouver for the spring. You weren't as careful as you should have been. You were three weeks late.

Of course, you couldn't (neither of us could, really) be seen buying pregnancy tests in the commissary. There were none to be obtained there without your parents—God help us—knowing about it. So you called us. I thought I would let you talk to my dad on your own, but you were shy, and wanted me there. He sat next to you on the couch in his study and told you everything was going to be okay. Do you remember his flat fingernails? Do you remember the freckled scalp shining under his thinning, feathery hair; do you remember the sweet smell of his deodorant as he squeezed your shoulders? You were happy to tell him what had happened. To enter the bathroom and pee into the plastic cup that would go in his briefcase, happy to come back the following week to receive the news, happiest of all to throw your arms around his neck when he told you there was nothing to worry about. Happy to close our door behind you.

Maha,

My dad didn't know who I was two weeks before he died. One morning he reached out and touched my left breast, thinking perhaps that I was one of the pretty nurses. Or maybe an old girlfriend: someone he knew he'd loved once, but couldn't remember when or in what way. Or how much.

Oh Maha,

Why couldn't you have said one word that would have let me forgive you? Maha, why didn't you?

The End of Summer

Chris Anderson

In the morning now I hear the call
of the Swainson's thrushes flying low

on the edge of the dark: *weep weep weep*.
Summer is done. Every morning

is darker and darker, and they are leaving,
they are leaving, carrying away

their summer song, and the moon is coming
through the oak tree, and the air

is fresh and sweet. You have to wake up early.
You have to stand on the porch and strain

to hear them, above the rumble of the semis
shifting up out of town. The morning stars

are singing. *Weep weep weep*. Sometimes
there are hundreds of thrushes, a river

of thrushes. Sometimes I am so afraid
of dying. Sometimes I think

I never will.

In his next life he'll excavate tree bark

Angela Heiser

if words were powerful enough to reincarnate at will
I'd speak you back to breathing, heart beating
back where I can fit you between my wings
and introduce you to my downy ducklings
over a few dozen maple glazed doughnuts
what did you say to the fairies?
did the moon really transport your thoughts to me?
thoughts germinated when you were alone tending to your beloved forests
measuring trees and maintaining trails for the packs of testy tourists each season
my National Park Ranger, where are you now that my lonely ears can't hear you anymore?
I am entirely at the mercy of a sneaky woodpecker drilling *who are you?* just out of my reach—
I realize it's you in your airborne form watching me and I smile up at the canopy, bereft, but not alone

Ode to a Standing Hair Dryer

—after Donald Justice

Lee Rossi

There it stood
in the basement corner
all the winters of my childhood
this spinster, thin as metal tubing
her glittering swollen bonnet
jaw unhinged like an anaconda
ready to receive the supplicant heads
of older women, hair wrapped in plastic
rollers or coiled and flattened
with bobby pins. What miracles
she wrought, my mother,
all the springs of my youth,
transforming parched and arid acres
into gleaming golden fields,
a brush, a comb, a bottle of mist,
a can of spray,
the anxious dryer leaning nearby
guard and confidant, angel and mantis,
her artist's conscience.
Once in the summer of my innocence,
I placed my delicate head

newly shorn into that rattling maw,
and saw what the others saw,
what my mother knew
and hid from me, a law
that held no justice, only dread.

The Gardens of Schönbrunn

Ellie Lange

I met Gisella Bartolomé the morning I dropped my violin bow into the Naiad fountain in Schönbrunn Gardens.

Well, not so much dropped, but threw.

I'm not usually so erratic. Violinists aren't supposed to be violent and unpredictable; they're graceful and demure and would never dream of throwing their $20,000 bow into the leaf-laden waters of a palace fountain. I wasn't even supposed to bring my violin into the expansive gardens surrounding Schönbrunn. I wasn't supposed to be playing violin at all.

All I wanted was to prove to myself that I could still play. I'd been to the gardens before—many times, in fact—and I'd watch accordionists and flutists play romantic Mozart serenades and move passersby to tears. These moments were so beautiful I almost believed that while I could no longer play in a professional symphony orchestra, I could handle busking in a public garden.

I opened my case on a bench near the fountain, its waters speckled with stray Euro coins, autumn leaves, and the occasional blush of algae. My hands began trembling. I persisted anyway, untucking my violin from its velvet blanket, slipping on the shoulder rest, wiping rosin off the strings, untightening the bow, rosining it vigorously after months of disuse. Once revived, I brought my instrument to my shoulder. Around me, a few tourists in jean shorts and fanny packs milled about. One girl, perhaps twelve, watched me as I plucked my fingers haphazardly across the strings. She abruptly stopped alongside the path to the fountain for several moments before her mother pulled her out of my sight into the blinding noontime sun.

With no one paying attention, I tried to bring my bow to the string and pull it effortlessly across like I had thousands of times before. But it was as if a magnetic force entered my violin, froze my forearms. I could do nothing but stand still, violin on shoulder and bow in the air, as unmoving as the marble statue before me. I took a moment to study it. The giant marble bird in the fountain's central sculpture made no sound as a woman and child stood nonchalantly atop its feathered body. Beneath them, the bird squawked silently in pain, beak forever agape. Nineteen months ago, I was the only one frozen in stone, not the violator straddling my abdomen, free to do whatever they pleased to my body.

Suddenly, my violin started to feel like a violation to my body, too, digging without permission into the bony crevices of my shoulder.

This time, unlike my first experiences of assault, I couldn't help but scream. I yanked the foreign body from my shoulder, jerked my arm with the bow toward the water, and released my hand. Out flew the bow, plopping fantastically into the water of the Naiad Fountain.

For a moment, I stood there in shock, watching my $20,000 stick of rosewood and horsehair float haphazardly in the pale, autumnal-splotched water. My former conductor, whose name I can no longer speak aloud, would say that a true violinist would never throw their instrument into the water; it would be physically impossible for that instinct to take over. Well, I don't know if he'd say that or not; this situation had never occurred before. But either way, I knew he'd think me even crazier if he saw me there, throwing one of my prized possessions into a public fountain.

With that realization, all I did was stand there, frozen, as my bow floated daintily in the murky waters. Nothing could be solved by immediately fishing it out. The damage was already done. I'd have to take it to the luthier regardless or perhaps simply get rid of it altogether. A financial loss, to be sure, but one that savings from five-years' salary in the Boston Symphony Orchestra, and my instrument's insurance, would easily cover. I glanced around, wondering if any passersby had witnessed my moment of insanity, although the few still meandering off in the distance appeared not to notice. I listened to the soft grind of footsteps against the gravel, the birds twittering above, mocking my terrible impulsiveness. Beside me, the fountain gurgled, and I turned to see the marble woman and child basking in their triumph as they continued to suffocate the bird.

"Are you going to take care of that? Or should I?"

An Austrian voice entered the mix. I spun around to find a small woman wearing a gingham bucket hat and tall olive rubber boots. She was petite, only five feet, maybe even less. Her dark, wavy hair jutted out in all directions from the sweat-stained gingham hat.

"I..." I croaked, but I guess the shock—or embarrassment—was still too much, for no other words came out. My cheeks were already impossibly red from the beating sun, and they only continued to deepen in color.

"I'll get it." She switched to English. My clumsiness must have betrayed my Americanness.

I noticed the woman's gardening shears and the bits of twigs poking out from her thick raven's nest of hair. She didn't look like any of the gardeners I'd encountered here before. For starters, they were all men. Perhaps she was also doing an illegal service for the patrons of Schönbrunn, just as I had hoped to by attempting to play without a permit.

Sauntering right up to the fountain, she reached her rusty gardening shears toward the center, instantly plucking up my beloved bow in its metallic fangs. Droplets of water shuddered down from the wood like a wet dog shaking its tail, and I resisted the urge to gasp.

She was kind enough not to drop the bow on the sandy ground, instead gently placing it in my free outstretched hand. It felt like a slimy wet fish in my sweaty palm, and I was careful to keep its moistness from infecting my violin.

"Thank you," I whispered, but when I looked up from my bow, she was already gone, leaving behind only a scented trail of dahlia perfume. As I looked closer at the path she exited on, I noticed a slight silver glint that had not been there before. A bracelet, I discovered upon further inspection. I set down my violin in its case to pick it up. A single band of vegan leather, the edges fraying slightly, imprinted with a dainty floral design, pressed together with a single silver clasp. It was likely homemade or bought cheap at a market, yet I felt strangely drawn to it all the same. Perhaps because it smelled faintly of dahlia perfume.

I pocketed the leather bracelet. A part of me wanted to keep it for a reason I couldn't place. The other part wanted to return it just like my bow had miraculously been returned to me.

Either way, I prayed I would find its owner, the rescuer of my bow, again.

I lost Gisella Bartolomé's leather bracelet the same evening I said goodbye to her for good. The same leather bracelet that I'd picked up that fateful autumn afternoon.

I found her in the gardens two weeks after the infamous fountain incident. I was already wearing the bracelet on my wrist. She'd marched right up to the bench where I was reading and said that she recognized me as the violinist who dropped her bow in the fountain. She instantly noticed her vegan leather bracelet on my wrist, and I blushed. Before I could offer to return it, she told me to keep it, as long as I told her my name. I did. Anni. And that's how our friendship began.

Four months later, the bracelet was gone. I lost it only a couple of hours before I realized I'd never see her again. That day, Vienna was as frigid and cold as her people, and an icy February cold front bathed the city in frost. I should have known something bad was coming. Gisella was always encouraging me to trust my intuition. Had I done so, perhaps I might not have lost her, Gisella Bartolomé, keeper of the English oak trees, vegan leather enthusiast, Austrian native, youngest thirty-five-year-old I'd ever met, love of my life.

I was in too much of a hurry, however, to keep track of the vegan leather bracelet on my wrist, let alone listen to that tugging feeling that I should go back to Gisella's little flat in the fifth district and take her up on her peace offering, two tickets to the Vienna Philharmonic. Prior to this evening, we hadn't spoken for fourteen days. I'd upset her, I knew. So I gave her space. Then, she called me out of the blue, about five hours before the concert, asking me if I'd come with her. No other context, no mention of our fight two weeks ago. Simply asking for a night at the orchestra.

I said no. I'd do anything but that. That or try to play my violin again. She hung up. I went to her flat and pounded on the door and begged for forgiveness. She opened the door, flung the two Vienna Philharmonic tickets at my chest, and slammed it shut again. I waited for two hours for her to change her mind and let me back in. She didn't, so I left.

Somehow, close to eight o'clock, I found myself lingering near the Musikverein, home of Vienna's famous philharmonic. I stood outside the U-Bahn station. Icy gusts of wind dashed between Baroque-style buildings, darting beneath my fraying wool coat. I watched the glowing gold and scarlet music hall impatiently awaiting me across the street. Throngs of people passed by me, clearly on their way to see the Philharmonic, chattering excitedly in German and English and Slavic languages I couldn't decipher. Like the audacious winter wind, something pulled me toward the hall that night. I resisted it.

Instead, as eight dawned upon me, I remained outside the station, tucked inside the overhang away from the bitter cold next to a homeless man covered in a tent of camouflage blankets. I couldn't physically hear the Vienna Philharmonic all the way over here, not with the clacking of Fiaker horse-drawn carriages and cars rumbling by. I didn't need to physically hear it, however, to feel the music in my soul. It had been exactly eighteen months since I'd heard the opening tuning, the buzzing excitement dripping from just a few haphazard notes, and yet, I could hear it perfectly now: the muffled German as the announcer asked for audience members to turn off their cell phones, the shuffling of black-flat clad feet, the rustling of the conductor's tuxedoed sleeves. The sweet, perfect major chord opening of Mozart's Symphony No. 41, springtime blossoming from the violins like bees buzzing around a daffodil, the occasional cough sprinkled in. It all swirled with the city's own symphony, the homeless man humming the Blue Danube beside me, the clacking of white horses as they carried tourists along the streets, a child's pure, Austrian-accented voice floating on top.

I heard it all, this beautiful symphony, real and imagined, and I wanted to cry. I knew I couldn't, though. I hadn't been able to cry in the eighteen months since I left the orchestra and gave up violin. Ever since then, intertwined with every note I heard, I saw him, too. His empty brown eyes bearing into mine as he slammed my body to the ground. His hands as he clenched my neck while he inserted himself inside me, once only forty minutes after we'd finished playing the Schubert Symphony No. 8, once while he played Schubert's Symphony No. 1 on his old record player. Other times, I'd be the one actively playing, some Mozart or Shostakovich orchestral excerpt for a "private coaching," when I'd feel his hands start to grope my chest.

I saw him, felt him, there too, even as I stood several feet away from the Musikverein. I didn't need to hear the music, to touch my own violin, to be reminded of its violation.

I took one sharp breath, and closed my eyes, trying to picture Gisella instead.

Gisella.

Maybe someday, I told myself, I'd tell her the full story. Tell her why I don't play the violin anymore, why I can't go to the Vienna Philharmonic or to any orchestra concert. Tell her that no, I didn't quit the violin because I was passed up for principal second violin and I was burnt out and tired of always sitting in the back.

But I knew that if I told her the truth, I could never face her again. I could hardly face myself anymore. Couldn't face anyone who knew the real version of Anni, the one who had been assaulted countless times and allowed it to continue happening for the sake of her career. Until, in the end, she was fired anyway.

That's why I didn't turn around and hop on the U-Bahn back to her quaint flat in the fifth district, apologize and tell her she's right, let's go to the symphony together tonight.

As the sound of rapturous applause stirred in my mind, I brushed my wrist. A pang pierced my chest as I realized it was empty. My bracelet, Gisella's bracelet. It must have fallen off on the U-Bahn, on the way to this cursed concert hall.

I hopped back on the U4 line to Margareten, my head pulsing. How could I be so stupid to not clasp it tighter? I cursed my absent-mindedness.

When I arrived at Gisella's flat, all I could think about was my bracelet and the nauseating A theme of Mozart's 41st symphony. I rapped on the building's peeling, hyacinth-purple front door, and when no one answered, I unlocked it with the key she'd given me two months ago. I hiked up the three flights of white marbled, winding stairs, still hyper-fixated on the bracelet and not on the fact that I couldn't hear Gisella's blaring television. It wasn't until I opened the door to Apartment 15 and saw the note on her counter that I realized.

I didn't scream, or cry, or sink to the floor, or anything. I merely stood there, frozen as the city of Vienna at that moment, replaying the same four opening bars of the symphony in my mind, wondering if some strange passerby had picked up my leather bracelet by now.

Gisella told me she'd never had a first kiss when we were drinking Wiener Melanges at Café Sperl.

"I'm sick, you see," she told me in her beautiful, Austrian-accented English. We always spoke in English, for despite my semi-proficient German, Gisella insisted on practicing her English. "I never had time for love, even before it progressed. Now I don't have the energy."

What is this right now, I wanted to say, if not love? But I didn't. Instead I asked, "What do you mean, you're sick?"

She told me. It was only our fifth encounter together, and I'd asked her to get coffee with me, as I had this silly checklist of hitting all the famous cafes in Vienna. Café Sperl was supposed to be a hidden gem. Traditional, with sparkling chandeliers and waiters dolled up in tuxedos, with Apfel Strudel and Melanges and Hauskuchen and a pleasant mix of murmuring German and echoing English. It was tucked away in the sixth district, further away from the boisterous American tourists in the city center. We could talk for hours on end there without fear of swarms of tourists.

And talk for hours we did. It was that sort of conversation that meandered endlessly through trivial topics such as the composition of Viennese coffee to deeper ones like how I ended up in Vienna and what it was like to live with a progressing chronic illness.

"Will you teach me to garden?" I asked her.

She took a sip of her Melange, leaving behind a little dollop of froth on her upper lip as she tenderly set the cup on the table.

"It's like music, really," she told me. She knew music was one of the few things I understood. "But you use your nose instead of your ears."

"I always thought gardening was more with your hands."

"Sometimes, when all you want is a pretty flower or perfectly trimmed bush. But close your eyes and take a deep breath. What do you smell?"

I did as Gisella told me. I always did exactly as she told me. I closed my eyes and inhaled. I smelled coffee beans roasting. The faint musk of wool, from a coat only recently taken out of summer storage. Something buttery, like my father's kitchen when he'd made his famous gourmet grilled cheese. A dash of jasmine, of leather, of all sorts of perfumes and colognes mingling together. And almost imperceptible, the smell of horse manure mixed with rain, lingering from the cobblestone outside.

"Doesn't that make this café come alive?" Gisella asked.

I nodded.

"I always pick which flower to plant based on my nose first, then my eyes. It's no different than composing a symphony. A bassline of cedar mulch, then the pink roses soaring over with the melody; unison strings. Baby's breath, the breathy flute icing the top, the descant. Lamb's ear the harmony. You breathe in, you can smell the symphony."

Symphony. The word pricked my chest.

"Ah, yes," was all I could say. Nothing more beautiful than a symphony.

"Are you going to join an orchestra here in Vienna?" she asked me. I'd already told her I used to play for the Boston Symphony Orchestra for three years before I decided to move to Vienna a year ago. When she asked why Vienna, I told her it was to feel closer to my late mother, who studied abroad there in college and apparently talked about it nonstop after that, according to my father. That was partially true. The real reason was to run as far away as possible from Boston, from all the people in my previous life, including my father. A phone call a week to him was the only connection to my old life.

"No," I said, circling back to her question about the orchestra. "I've given up all that."

She swiped the froth from her lip, forehead wrinkling in confusion. She wanted to ask more questions, I could tell. How do you go from being a tenured violinist in one of the world's top orchestras, job security for life, to working as a receptionist?

"I see. Career change?" she asked.

"Something like that." I held the cup at my lips for several seconds, despite it being completely empty of coffee. "Hey, have any job openings at Schönbrunn? I'm getting sick of sitting at a desk all day." I chuckled. Gisella did not.

"Well, you can take my job."

"Are you going full-time at your other job?" Gisella worked two jobs. One for Schönbrunn, and another for the city government tending to the parks.

"More like becoming a full-time invalid."

Oh. For a moment, I'd forgotten she was sick.

"It's progressing, then?" I asked.

Gisella nodded. "I'm lucky I've been able to keep working for this long. I'm handing in my notice next month."

"I'm sorry."

"At least it's not terminal. Just something I must live with for the rest of my life." Gisella sighed, then continued. "I've never been in love, but I never really cared because at least I was pursuing my lifelong dream." The next part didn't escape her lips. It was silent, implicit. *And now, my dreams are gone.*

I knew what it meant to give up on your dreams, especially when that's all you had. Only, mine was a choice. Hers wasn't.

Gisella kissed me for the first time in Stephansplatz.

She'd quit all her gardening jobs one month ago, before the autumn blooms entered their winter slumber. Twenty-eight days ago, she'd begun her own sort of slumber, a post-treatment hibernation as she hid away in her bed in her fifth district flat. I'd seen her every day in that time, bringing the latest Emily Henry or Ann Patchett novel to read, my favorite beginner's embroidery kit of her favorite flowers, a Melange to-go from the rare café that offered such American laziness. Her mother wanted her to move in with her, in the Tyrol region of Austria several hours away. Gisella was too weak, she said, to live on her own. What if she was too exhausted to get out of bed to eat? What if she fainted in the shower?

Gisella, however, wanted nothing more than to stay here. I wanted nothing more than for her to stay here. So I promised I'd be the one to take care of her, to essentially move in.

As long as I have you, she told me, *I'm not going anywhere.*

And that's how I became her primary caretaker, although she didn't need much, except someone to make sure she was okay.

Today, Gisella wanted to go out. To see people. She was finally feeling up to it, and the sun bathed the city in a warm winter bliss. I suggested a café visit; she demanded Stephansplatz. If you go out to be around people, why not choose the busiest plaza in the city?

We sat on a bench in the corner of the cathedral's plaza, staring out at the masses of pigeons and tourists snapping photos of the looming Gothic church beside us, saying nothing. A few meters away, an accordionist belted out *Eine Kleine Nachtmusik*. I didn't even realize I was tapping my left hand along to the sonorous melody until I felt Gisella's hand stroke mine. She took mine in hers, cradling it like an injured bird, lifting each finger one by one and studying it as if it were one of the swallows she liked to observe back when she gardened at Schönbrunn.

"You must have been told you'd make a perfect pianist as a child," she murmured. "Your fingers, they are so long, so graceful."

I nodded, noticing my pointer fingernail still had a fleck of pale pink polish, not quite rubbed off. I wonder if Gisella felt the calluses on my pads, or if they were scarcely noticeable anymore. After all, they hadn't brushed a string since that botched performance in Schönbrunn.

"You wouldn't even play the accordion, if I asked?"

"No." After a moment of silence, I added. "I'd do anything else for you, though. I hope you know that."

"Will you kiss me?"

I jerked my hand away, inadvertently. The question had never even been posed before, not in gazes, not in between compliments on my smile and anecdotes of cute couples, not nestled in between the cobblestone of all the romantic scenery Vienna possessed.

"I've never been kissed before, and I want to know what it's like. That's all."

I nodded. I'd been there, too, at twenty-one. So I placed my hand back in her open palm, leaned over, and gently kissed her on the lips. She laughed, her long hair wavering uncontrollably in the wind.

"Now we are true friends."

I taught Gisella Bartolomé how to play the violin on her thirty-sixth birthday.

For her present, she'd asked me to show her how to play the violin. I would've rather done anything else, but when I first refused, she went quiet for several hours, and I'd never seen her look so hurt. Eventually, I relented. It was her birthday, after all.

We stood near the Naiad Fountain in the center of Schönbrunn Gardens, the place where we'd first met almost four months ago. I'd somehow managed to get my bow repaired at the luthier since then, and we stood far away from the spray of the fountain, instead under a bareboned tree where we were somewhat shielded from the playful evening breeze. The moon was a thumbprint in the sky, barely peeking out from the streaks of clouds leftover from an odd February thunderstorm. Gisella had trimmed this tree for her last day of work, and its perfectly sculpted branches stood guard for us, upright as the Viennese Polizei, only this tree promised not to tattle on us for breaking into the gardens after closing.

I removed my violin from its case, slowly lifting it up to Gisella's bony left shoulder. She nodded, giving her silent permission for me to sculpt her posture to the demands of the instrument. Gently, I raised her chin, then brushed a lock of her wavy hair, soft as a roasted chestnut, off her shoulder. The violin nestled effortlessly between the soft flesh of her chin and the black satin fabric covering her shoulder. Slowly, I eased her chin back down and molded her left arm around the fingerboard of the violin. I could feel her muscles trembling, her breath shaking. We knew this wouldn't be easy for her. But she wanted to come here, to hold the violin, all the same. And though it pained me to touch my instrument, I couldn't say no to Gisella.

"I'm getting tired. Can we take a break?"

"Of course."

I took the violin back.

"Can you play me something? A serenade, perhaps?" Her eyes were big, two round thumbprints like the moon. I almost couldn't resist. Almost.

"You know I can't do that." I laughed, but it came out breathier than I had hoped, as wispy as the baby's breath.

"Why not?"

I sucked in my breath. "Gisella, please."

"You can open up to me, you know. You can trust me."

"No, I can't." It came out sharper than I intended, but I just wanted this conversation to end.

Gisella bit her lip. "I just want to help you, Anni. I can tell you're unhappy and that you want to play again, and I—"

And then I snapped. "Just because you can't continue your dream, doesn't mean the rest of us have to, no matter what expense."

Gisella stared at me for a moment with those big round, thumbprint eyes. Then, shakily, she rose from the bench, frail as the withering branches of the tree beside us, and she walked away.

That was the first time I realized I might never see her again.

When I walked into Gisella's empty apartment the night of the Vienna Philharmonic concert, I found a note on the entryway table, and I realized she had left for good.

How she had managed to leave in the few hours I'd been gone, I don't know. Perhaps her mom, who I suspected had already replaced me as her caregiver, had helped her. She had to have already packed even before she called me. Perhaps a part of her already knew that I'd say no. Perhaps her plan had always been to leave, and she only wanted to give me a last chance to convince her to stay.

I collected myself and took one final stroll through the flat I'd been to countless times.

Before, I'd described her place simply as Gisella—overflowing with green, more plants than a greenhouse, and the occasional old *Vogue* cover or *Parisian* magazine on the wall. Now, it was simply white. Sterile hallway, kitchen empty of coffee grounds on the counter, living room suffocating under the absence of plants. All white, except for a single, black napkin, words scrawled on it in silver sharpie.

Gone home. You should too.

Love,

G

The morning after I realized Gisella had left Vienna for good, I knew where I had to go.

That morning, dawn must have whispered some sort of magic spell to the gardens of Schönbrunn, for everything itched with the glowing promise of spring. I found my spot next to the Naiad fountain, violin case clutched in my hand. This time, I had no desire to toss my bow into the murky water of the fountain.

Instead, I withdrew it from its case, just as I had with Gisella that one fateful evening. I clutched the bow firmly in my right hand, the violin nestled perfectly on my left shoulder, and I drew a note. One single note. An opening, tuning A.

I put my case away and said goodbye to the gardens of Schönbrunn.

Orb Weaver at My Writing Cabin

Sydney Lea

That spider sheds no tears,
doesn't laugh or speak.
It appears so calm, all workaday,
as it conceives its web.

I stand a while to watch it fashion
an artful construct that's also a jail
that will hang from a wooden eave.
If I impute something like *soul* to the creature,

it's because I can't help myself.
To insist that the creature finds joy in creation,
joy laced with sorrow—that's my own misprision,
I know. The web will be rebuilt

each day but in time will vanish,
becoming a pallid smear
against this small drab structure I enter
for foredoomed attempts

at matching the spider's resourcefulness.
(Indulge my calling it genius or such.)
We both find ourselves on the verge of winter,
whose storms are bound to undo so much.

enchiridion rushing into the hurricane

Lisa Lewis

if I piloted a drone above an interstate highway
like a knife edge slicing a mountain next to a ravine

if I released a bottle of black beetles into a flooded house
like a grave full of ocean full of sky

if I climbed over fallen trees to scale what used to be a road
like a little river   a mud path floating sticks

I wouldn't say any of these things

I wasn't born there   it's a story of the past I decided not to tell
it makes us all look bad   shitkickers and abusers
turning the car off to save gas on the crusade down the mountain
with that geometric swaying to the harmony of the curves
it wasn't safe, the power steering didn't work so it took strength
to grip on to the road   what if we flew would the trees catch us
would the trees hold out their crackling arms
would the trees catch fire

at my undergraduate school the annual Biltmore House visit
was a big deal for the mountain girls like me who didn't take many trips

we were led into a library with ladders and velvet chairs
it makes you imagine those things for yourself
a mansion taking a mountainside
settling across the ridge to pry the moon out of its slot

let's not forget why I'm talking about this

torrent beside I-40 where are the trees?
covered? by raging waters over their tallest tips?
pines covered   pines pines pines   highway's edge
racing along the top   I have been there racing
and swaying I remember it with my arms
and my hands gripping the wheel

why does it feel now I should not be speaking about this

nothing at stake but the past and the strained ability to love
the unknown dead in a time of unrest
in a city that seemed above me every way
my little car aching under the gas pedal
on the drive up from Lenoir and back in a single day
because teenagers are supposed to be home for dinner
the same tall pines frowned behind the big ugly house
lost in the bankruptcy suit

to return requires pushing through what I already pushed away

enchiridion rushing into the hurricane

once driving from Charlotte with a guy I worked with
he took out his enormous penis and fondled it
for my viewing pleasure   that was all his
I kept my eyes on the road   the eighteen-wheelers
the curvaceous runaway escape ramps rippled with sand
what was the use   what was the use   no use not today

once I released a jar full of fleas in a house trailer
because the man who lived there had tried to set up a gangbang
it would've happened if a friend hadn't overheard
the planning
the worst was   as always   *I thought he liked me*
you have to learn not to trust what rushes down the dirt roads
you learn to set aside tendencies towards generosity
wherever they came from   someone's well-intended childhood lesson

now no one knows how many are still lying around like rotting logs
bodies corpses old hillbillies people like my ancestors
too many children old broken hickory   old gravel descendants
somewhere in cabins or streams
some say there's no smell here   they make videos to say it
some say the figures can't be released because so many chainsaws
the young long-faced guy with the huge dick
is someone else now   someone with a friendly but crushed
Labrador Retriever   someone else with a camp stove and a knife

enchiridion: a word I looked up today
it contains essential information on a subject
and the subject may be floods or storms

I may turn out to write the enchiridion
or it might be one of the angry faces in videos
shouting about FEMA   or it might be one of the roofs
like paper cups bobbing in a gutter

there is no "last storm"
the next one is always larger
my undergraduate school went out of business
here a thousand miles from Asheville
I hold a yardstick to the pillars in my living room
and measure two lines

I don't know what either of them means
about next time

Ruby's Eighth

Molly Best Tinsley

It begins like any day that summer. Mom, in her eye-mask and some boyfriend's T-shirt, working on sleep. Ruby and me lying on the shady patch of grass behind the apartment, with nothing to do but claim clouds.

I point to a puffy one floating overhead and call, "Curled-up cat."

Ruby drags my arm down, points at the exact same fluff, and shouts, "Camel with no legs."

"Sorry," I say, "but I was first."

"Cats do not have humps, Pearl. Camels do. Too bad someone cut its legs off," Ruby adds, also claiming the last word.

I tried for it once, and she started throwing punches.

She was sort of a pain, my half-sister. Anything to cause trouble.

On school days, if I said, "Hurry or we'll miss the bus," she put on the brakes. Then we'd have to trudge back home up all those stairs, me lugging my bookbag, Ruby swinging figure eights with her empty second-grade pretend one.

Mom would open the door wrapped in her shiny bathrobe, then holler to whichever boyfriend was lolling somewhere behind her: "Time to haul ass out of here and drop my family jewels at school."

I did like being called a jewel, and I knew it was thanks to cute Ruby, with her red-orange curls and plump mouth. I was plain Pearl, with straight brown hair so thin my ears poked through like dried apricots or something. Plus all the boyfriends had shiny trucks, and I liked leaping off the running board when we got to school then helping Ruby down by the hand while the kids still on the bus crowded the windows to stare.

Anyway, when school was on, Mom forgot lunch money sometimes and teacher conferences always. But she knocked herself out for our birthdays. And the July day I can't forget, with its ordinary start, is about to turn special because it's Ruby's eighth. I still don't understand out how special turned into something else.

Mom's invited all the boyfriends to a big party, and they haul in fancy decorated cakes and put on magic shows. They do handstands where there's barely space and let Ruby and me have the coins that drop from their pockets. They dance the tango with Mom up and down the hall, breaking things as they swoop into the living room.

The guy named Rick shows up last. His long legs march through the door ahead of the rest of him, followed by a bulging pillowcase on his back. He's been sleeping over with Mom lately, so I think maybe it's dirty laundry. But then why is he clutching it on his lap through all the cake and champagne and tricks?

Everyone around the table is pretty zonked, except for the burping, when he pushes back his chair and lets the pillow case fall open around a pile of thick coils. His wrists bulge as he works with both hands to get a grip on them. Then with a grunt, he stretches them out over his head and yells, "Boa constrictor!"

Mom and I scream and the boyfriends lurch to their feet. But Ruby? She's been sitting beside Rick, and now she's jumping around grabbing at the tail end twisting over her head. When he lowers the snake to writhe on his lap, she keeps trying to hug it until Mom finally yanks her away. Then to be polite, Mom inches back to Rick and gives the thing a pat, so I do too. It's not that bad, just weird, the way something ripples under its smooth, cool skin.

To be honest, Rick's surprise sort of kills what's left of the party spirit. One too many champagne tastes sends me to sprawl on the sofa, and through the fog, I watch the boyfriends stumble out the door, all but one I don't recognize, who's helping Mom wash the glasses. Then he starts cramming gooey cardboard plates and tangled crepe paper into the big, black bag she holds open, and I come to enough to ask, "Where's the snake?"

"Gone forever, I hope," Mom says. Then her brow pinches as she looks around at the mess. "Where is your sister?"

I shrug.

"Check your bedroom," she snaps and tromps out onto the landing to peer down the stairwell. I take one shaky step toward the hall before she changes her mind. "Go see if Rick's truck is still there."

"Where?" I ask.

"Out. Just go. And don't dawdle."

Insulted, I take my time on the stairs. Besides, in my state, wouldn't it have been dangerous to rush?

Outside the night's still hot. As far as my eyes can see in the dark, a million cars are parked front-in along the curb. I can't breathe, I feel dizzy, but I make myself shuffle down the sidewalk, until I bump into the backend of a truck. A stinky cloud of exhaust sort of belches from underneath, and my heart gives a hard, scared thump.

The truck starts to move. I scream Rick's name then Ruby's, take a flying leap off the curb and another onto its running board. I hang onto the locked door handle long enough to punch the passenger window then fall into the street.

The truck backs up to where I'm collapsed and trying to decide if I broke my arm. Then the window slides down, and above me, I hear Ruby chirp, "Go home, Pearl."

"I need to take you with me," I call, struggling to sit myself up.

Ruby's curls bloom in the dark. "Wow, Pearl, what happened to your legs?"

"I hurt my arm," I say.

"Rick's taking just me to a carnival, OK?" Ruby says. "I'm gonna learn to be a snake charmer," she adds, before the truck starts rolling forward again and her pale cloud of a face floats away forever.

The Walk

Paul Rabinowitz

if time is measured in a cigarette
the seconds to walk from my car to the cafe

the burn of the first puff of white smoke
to the black ash crushing at the end

to watch you pour intricate patterns
from steamed milk

I wonder if it's easier to just strike a match
light a cigarette

adjust the six-gun slung low at my hip
kick the mud from my boot

as I dismount
strap my horse to the hitching post

sunburnt and sore I lengthen my gait
push open the doors

The Walk

hear the frenzied rhythm of poets
tapping wildly on keyboards

watching me as I cross the dusty tile floor
scanning the room for outlaws

stepping up to the counter I meet your eyes halfway
as you lean forward

an untamed curl falls from behind your ear
and suddenly the tapping stops

I unsnap the pearl button of my leather vest
you reach under the counter for a box

I pull out a cigarette
you strike the phosphorus tip setting the match ablaze

white smoke swirls between us
I tuck the curl behind your ear

we speak about downward facing dog
nutritional superfoods

the bio-sourced lavender fragrance of your shampoo
sun salutation at moon rise

I straighten my back and remove my Stetson
the gash on my forehead still raw

The Walk

a fight with a cattle-hand who warned me
to stay away   cafes are for poets

I extinguish my cigarette on the counter
tighten the holster 'round my hips

turn my body walk towards the exit   hear you shout
smoking is not allowed here

next time leave the chaps at home
just give me a poem to read on my break

when suddenly all hell breaks loose
the poets take aim

whistling western tunes while tapping away in unison
as if their life depended on it

Grayhairs at the Poetry Reading

Tim Gillespie

Where are all the young folks,
the bubbling-up poets,
the growing-into-their-words ones,
the strivers, the try-it-outers,
the make-it-newbies?

At their slams and jams:
noisy, finger-snapping,
head-bobbing, *yeah man*-ing,
call-and-response scenes.

Not here where we're careful:
hoarding words, telling it slant,
reciting yesterday's revolution—
free verse, tennis with no net—
to quiet, politely-dazed claps.

They're straighter shooters,
these young guns—in love
with sounds, hip-hop rhythms,
internal rhymes; I know the labels,
they've got the chops. Their

poems are performance, politics,
profane guts and grace and energy.

Here it's a lot of poems
about flora and fate,
small sniffs of wisdom,
the only meter mortality.

Ah, fuck it.
That camellia I saw
on my quiet walk today
was blooming in December.

Main Line Fibonaccis

Linda and Bob Blatz

The
non-
addict,
logical
cognitive brain thinks,
"Arrest will teach her a lesson."
Not an active function in the brain of an addict.
Penality is not a deterrent, and don't call it a correctional system.
"Tough love will teach her a lesson." By whose logic does abandoning
her to fend for herself at the mercy of other addicts make sense?

You
use.
At least
you get a
break from you. We don't.
Parents and loved ones never know
what the next moment will bring, always on the alert.
I fear I'll have one glass too many only to get the late-night call from
the police.

Linden against Flame

Ita Lenane

—for Lillian Ignatius (Ktunaxa First Nation)

We sat in a vacant lot all night—
fried chicken in a bucket, two six packs
that you drank like water.
You all night too hot
in your T-shirt, me in my coat
wishing for coffee.
We told stories to each other.
When I ran out
you took over till the stories lit up
the horizon and the cops came.

I know your tribe holds stories closely.
Did you tell me some you shouldn't? Because
I don't remember even one, as if
guardians came and took them back. But
I remember how you linked them, hour after hour:
    "He was walking along and then—
        I don't know if it was the next
        day or if a thousand
        years

had passed, but
He was walking along…"

Your phone's been disconnected. I'm afraid
you've left us for the
rubber room
car crash
bedroom noose.

You emerged from boarding school improbably still fluent,
a native speaker under twenty. You'd drawn blood from the language
assassins and lay in armed ambush against all the others,
your linden against the dragon flame of everything.

We'd see each other at language conferences
on college campuses, where one morning
my uber driver said, as we passed
you walking along,
"I wooden wanna meet *that* in a dark alley:"

defiant hair, fisted hands,
eyes setting a distant
focal point on fire, blazing
yourself a trail. You had on
a brand new track suit,
softest mauve.

Having Faith in the Speed of Light

Judith Mikesch-McKenzie

i. Hypothesis/Question

We are the speed of light, she said, we have its
        properties. Sometimes we are ocean waves,
moving in pulses, building our power, but
        in a nanosecond, we are just a mote, dancing
randomly in the breeze through a window

we can speed away from others so fast that we
        seem to disappear, and then we can
dazzle them with all the colors we contain
        but mostly we are like light because
time and distance mean nothing to us at all.

ii. Confession

All the way up the hill, the argument
        dogged our steps—the first requirement
is contrition, we were told, but the one who
        disagreed argued that time is not the fourth
dimension, consciousness is, and while we
        spread our blanket on the hilltop, where
we could see that all that we'd ever known was
        visible and shining, they argued that time

must, god help us, end eventually, must—after
    all possible doings are done and done and
exhausted from so much doing—must simply
    lie down and mercifully, finally
just end.

iii. Observation/Hypothesis

Look, she said, the light from that cluster, that
    one over there, has been speeding towards
us, here on this hilltop, for so long that the light
    we are seeing now is eons old. Look at the
Milky Way, and you are looking back in time
    25,000 years—shift your gaze to Andromeda
and you see two million years in the past.
        [oh please, point to the beginning]
sad-smiling, she said, I can't, it's too far away
    and the light from the beginning has not
had time to reach us here on this hill, where
    the wet grass smells sweet, the darkness is
scented of campfires, and the whole universe
    glistens eternity above us as we wait
and watch our world igniting with fire.

iv. Contrition

Hearing this, those who propose contrition are
    sad, and even tender as they whisper:
perhaps light and time are entangled, are yin
    and yang, and your rules are
comic to them—not showing us past time,

but actually bringing the past to us
for us to justify and make right

so, okay, she answers, *I'll do confession.*
**are you contrite?*
I have regrets, she answers.
**but contrition?*
I take responsibility for what I've done, she says—
isn't that the same thing?
**No.*

v. Evidence/Data

She sits on the step, eyeing the shove where it leans against
the side of the house, where she left it hours ago
before the child came with her confession, her revelation,
she set the shovel there before the drive to the
hospital, before the tests, the talking, the release to bring
her home and then come to sit here, on the stoop,
wondering if perhaps he would wander by, he unaware
that she knows, and she thinks how easily the handle fits
her hand, how capable she is with its weight, and how
quickly she could reach him and never regret it at all

vi. Absolution

**no contrition?*
she: *I didn't do it, he never walked by*
**but you wanted to?*
she: *yes, I wanted to feel the impact. Repeatedly.*

**do you have contrition for that desire?*

she: *no.*

vii. Benediction for the End of Things

Sitting up on the blanket,
at the center, there's no light, said the child,
just darkness
the place of the beginning is the place where
at the moment of
creation, all things were flung away, and the
fastest of them
was light—speeding away, leaving us all
behind…don't look
for light at the place of beginning, what is
left there is quiet,
deep nothingness, and we can always point
to that.

viii. Penance/Proof

she settles back on the blanket, face
turned toward the glowing sky
above, and, a nanosecond away, her
mother begins to weep.

Winter Watercolor

—after a painting by Kimberly White

Jeanine Stevens

I walk this old road, skates over my shoulder,
look for a pond with perfect ice, but only
hairline cracks and small branches to trip me.

I'm awash in January: charcoal, oyster, porcelain—
that light that says no rain, no breeze, maybe snow.

A late in the day, hush-a-by quiet, scent
of car exhaust and gin. Oval pits of rabbit feet
lead elsewhere. My boots crunch in frozen mud.

Suddenly, bold shock of sun, hematite smear
leeches through slats of pink clouds,
a loud creaking, ice shifting, like whales
moaning escaping the fisherman's net.

I cross over a fallow field, join the tattered
scarecrow sinking to his knees in gratitude.

A Square of Muslin

Heather Hallberg Yanda

Outside a chateau—far
from my country, which is
addicted to war—one

branch-shaped shadow quivers
on my notebook's page, asks
me to include roses

in my poem: in a place
where it feels like nothing
goes wrong, wisteria

and roses share a stone
wall. Fibre artists, nearby,
discuss their work. Some threads

of their laughter weave through
the trees and reach me here,
where I have found solace—

from the Latin meaning
to comfort, though I hear
solar in the word too—

as if we require this
sunlight to achieve peace.
Mourning doves discuss their

grief; cicadas shake their
maracas. *We have two*
choices, Nature says: *we*

can be mired in the world's
hate or hold tightly this
love we find here, where we

see Time's light and hear
its music; we realize
its impermanence: we

will sew and write this time
with careful stitches, in
the mind's square of muslin.

Community Standards

Judith Mikesch-McKenzie

the blue fabric lifts listless in the dry desert air—its
motion barely detectable, its sky blue with hints
of pale pink offer a nod to the heat, and seem
relieved to drop back down

by a vote of seven to one, the community council
has banned hanging laundry outside—mindful,
they say, of the image the practice gives of our
neighborhood, 'cheapening all of us who
live and work here.'

the fabric settles back, concealing once more the image
of a woman and child, surrounded by a pile of
suitcases, bags and a few pots as they wait sitting
cross-legged on the hot sand

the comments offered in support painted the image
of wet clothes as more problematic than linen,
denim pants worn almost white, and work shirts
hanging upside down, sleeves dangling like
the thin arms of an eight-year old hanging from
a tree branch, laughing

three streets away in the ruined city, a news crew
    films a father and son crouched against a
building behind a slab of concrete, seeking shelter
    from the fighting soldiers when a sudden bullet
fells first the unarmed father, and then the
    small boy

seated on the metal folding chairs, a memory of
    the scent of wet percale infused with bleach
and bluing, all inhaled while walking down the
    threadcount canyon made by parallel lines
of bedsheets, leading to the safe playhouse built
    from unused linen, cradled against the back
of the house

at their makeshift home, the blue fabric scattered
    with soft pink flowers shudders slightly
where it hangs against the blasted concrete, and
    the woman bows her head, understanding.

On Fear

J. A. Stein

"Do I have the right
To be afraid?"
—James Tate

I

Once, in the afternoon reeds, I came upon a great egret. It was foraging in cordgrass, its tufted shape a brushstroke or flounce in a dream.

Nervously, it eyed me, perhaps a hundred yards down, and returned to its repast of killifish, minnows, small crabs—whatever tiny things it consumed.

On a detour from running, here in West Florida, I'd ventured out through the woods, traipsing beneath the tall slash pines, only to come upon a clearing, an estuary-field, as beautiful as any I'd seen...

II

2004

Sgt. Eyal Benin wore his boonie hat low on his brow, less like Beetle Bailey than a man who lived in fear of the sun. He was set to be discharged in several weeks. This stint, of being First Sergeant of an outfit of infantry conscripts in training, was probably the last thing he'd sought when enlisting. He had already fought down in Gaza, or so we were told, and despised training men even more.

One evening, I remember coming back from the latrine. It was just after nine, the one hour of rest that we had at *Bach Nahal*. Men were sewing buttons, greasing guns. A few lounged along their cots somewhat lazily, perhaps awaiting transfer—quite a few had requested to see the *kaban*, or army psychiatrist, a euphemism for moving to a noncombat role.

The moon glanced off the tarps, streaking the guy ropes that rustled along the chalk beds. Off in the distance, beyond a razor fence, the sharp peaks of the Negev glimmered beneath the night sky.

"Yehoshua—"

I stopped, raising my hand to salute him.

He didn't return it. The waning moon caught his eyes, which were a lustrous brown, nearly iridescent. "Gun goes in front at all times," he said in Hebrew, in words I'd barely come to understand (I was a volunteer from Chicago).

"*Ken, Ha'mefaked.*" Yes, commander.

Ignoring my salute, he trundled off to the tent for commanders, not even bothering to check that I was wearing my rifle in front of me, as required.

I wanted to slap him. Commanding a soldier, who'd come here of his own will and put up with this bullshit for over seven months, only to be rebuked like a newbie for hoisting his rifle while he pissed, was infuriating. I wanted to pick up the book he'd been carrying, a *Harry Potter* volume with a snowy-blue cover, and heave it to the tents, or, better yet, open fire at it with my M4.

But I knew he didn't care and was only doing what he saw as his job.

Or perhaps he detected in me the arrogance that come with being an American who's ventured overseas, only to replicate in pleasure what most Israelis are forced to endure (to say nothing of the Palestinians we'd soon be charged with oppressing, and about which I felt some ambivalence at best). That I hadn't had sex or eaten decent food or even sipped a glass of palatable wine in several months was probably of as much concern to him as the appearance of my gun, which, in rear position, represented less an aberration in the order of the world or an affront to his authority than a defect in character, and likely his as much as mine. It was as if to say that, yes, he knew his job here was bullshit, as was the Army's, and that all of us were just biding time, perhaps waiting to get killed, but at least we could try to act with some dignity in it, some measure of composure, and resolve.

I can recall his eyes glimmering, tinged faintly with the moon.

III

Outside my younger daughter's school in Mississippi, twenty years later, the sun beats down through the clouds. Having just emerged from the Fourth Grade Awards Ceremony, I'm shaking hands with the parent of her friend, a child who won nearly all of the awards (my daughter nabbed one in art, along with the A-B honor roll, about which I'm thrilled), when a shadow swoops over us, followed by a squawking groan.

A red-tailed hawk soars above, clutching something in its talons, possibly a starling. Another, likely its mom, trails them, emitting a fruitless squeak. They swerve past the oaks and disappear into the clouds. Another starling follows them, possibly the dad, and comes to rest on a flagpole, silhouetted by the sun.

I try to gauge the bird's expression. I try to avoid seeing a metaphor in it, with this feckless father sitting haplessly atop a still American flag as its offspring is being devoured, probably plucked and beheaded, on some feeding perch off in the east.

The other parent seems not to have noticed this. "We'll have you over for dinner," he adds. They're moving to the suburbs in June, and taking with them my daughter's best friend.

I am proud of my daughter. She's sometimes struggled in school, not for want of talent or intelligence. She's always been lonely, we know.

It isn't a question of race, though she's about the only "white" child in her grade. And it isn't a question of her attentiveness, which is admittedly flagging these days, as is true with most children, especially in an era of screens. Rather, it's her motivation, or perhaps her innate sense—which I can't say is wrong—that however much we study or try to connect, our lives become increasingly hard.

Last night, before bed, my daughter handed me a blood-flecked tooth, which she'd yanked from her jaw. "I think I should get five dollars for this one."

"I thought you didn't believe in the Tooth Fairy?"

"I believe in cash money." She smiled.

That evening, I searched in vain to find a five-dollar bill and wondered if I could write her a check. It also occurred to me that even if we wanted to move to the suburbs, it was doubtful that we could afford it these days.

IV

"Daddy, do you regret having served in the Israeli Army?" my older daughter asks me the next night over dinner. She's read in the news about the bombings in Gaza, with several-dozen Palestinians killed the past night.

"I don't know."

She spoons her peas. "I guess if you hadn't served, you wouldn't have met Mommy."

"This is true," I say, eying her plate. They know her mother and I met while living on a kibbutz, but that's about the extent of what we've said.

V

Although he's mainly known for his abstract painting and sculptures, Ellsworth Kelly, the American painter, was also a remarkable draftsman. I stumbled across an exhibition of his drawings in July of 2023.

In *Self-Portrait, Normandy, 1944,* Kelly, who was then eighteen and serving in the US Army's 603rd Engineer Camouflage Battalion, or "Ghost Army," as it was called, painted himself by candlelight in his tent. The plaque on the wall at the Art Institute described his *Self-Portrait,* which he scrawled in ink on a torn sheet of notepaper, as "haunting." The Museum's website elaborates: "The work conveys the isolation and fear the young Kelly must have felt amid such harrowing conditions." Yet the image struck me as less haunting than familiar, as if I've witnessed this face once before.

At first, it recalled an image I'd glimpsed the first night I'd enlisted, in 2004, in a barracks near Haifa, where I was awoken and told to stand guard. How I was to do this, much less communicate in a language I barely spoke, remains as much of a mystery to me today as it did at that time.

After struggling to lace my boots, I stumbled into the half-lighted murk of a bathroom, where a cracked mirror stood before me. I caught sight of myself in the glass. Wearing a green helmet and olive drab uniform, I wasn't sure who it was. Perhaps this is an experience that every soldier has.

In Kelly's *Self-Portrait,* the eyes are dim flecks, traced by the cone of a nose. Two jutting lips protrude sharply, both in stark relief. And the lip-shapes are perfect, despite the broad strokes, with the cupid's bow sagging, the philtrum pronounced, and the vermillion border slightly nubbed, as if chapped. It isn't fear that one detects in these features as much as simple truths: the unknowingness of war, the strange calm, the desperation.

"You like this one, Daddy?" asks my younger daughter, reaching for my arm.

She wears a purple fleece and white ski cap and smiles. She looks beautiful today, as she does every day. And the world is such a marvelous place.

I count my blessings to know her, and to have her, and to live.

"You promised we could get some hot cocoa," she adds. Her eyes are dark brown, though somewhat lighter than mine, and it occurs to me that I know whose steely portrait I now see.

VI

The obituary reported that shortly before his death, Sgt. Eyal Benin was accepted to study law at the Hebrew University of Jerusalem. It added that he was born in South Africa, which was shocking to read, because I'd never heard him speak English while serving.

Of course, that made sense, as only an anglophone immigrant would work that hard to conceal it.

When I first heard news of his death, which came in an email from one of my former platoonmates, I remember crawling along my blue sofa-bed, wondering if I could fly back from the U.S. to Israel and join the IDF reserves. As a foreign volunteer, I hadn't been obliged to do reserves, as most Israelis are until well into their mid-to-late forties.

Like Eyal, I was discharged from the IDF around the summer of 2005. But where he'd been called back for reserves—and apparently blown up along the border with Lebanon while patrolling in a Humvee in 2006—I'd remained in the U.S., content with pursuing a master's degree in creative writing. I was trying to write a novel, or something of the sort, and failing mightily at it, I knew.

The news reports of his death were difficult to parse; apparently two soldiers were captured from his Humvee and kidnapped into South Lebanon (Eyal wasn't one of them), which precipitated a violent response from the IDF. A thousand deaths later—mainly Lebanese, but also about a hundred Israelis—the IDF returned from Lebanon, less defeated than exhausted. Prisoners were swapped. Agreements were made. Several more from my brigade had been killed, as had a friend, a fellow American, but none of them would wrench me as Eyal's death still does. I'm still not entirely sure why.

VII

2025

My wife hates long car rides, and I like them even less, but the manatees, we know, are worth seeing.

Since Trump's election in 2024, my wife, who's a climate scientist and professor, has taken to rebranding herself an oceanographer. She knows little about oceans, she admits, with her specialties being atmospheric science and climate modeling. Yet recently her grants have been targeted, in some cases annulled, and there's talk of her field being banned. A former soldier herself (we met shortly after her discharge from the Israeli Air Force), she's more resigned than upset and less given to hostile musings than me.

When my younger daughter glances up from her iPad to ask once again how much longer until we're there, my wife gives her usual reply: "A couple weeks."

"What are the things that we're seeing?"

"Manadees," says our son, through a jumble of teeth (the Tooth Fairy is still in abeyance here).

"Are they like sharks?"

"They're mammals," says our son, who's studied them nightly in books with his mother—my younger daughter and I, meanwhile, have taken to reading about castles.

"I don't want to get bitten," she adds.

What my wife hasn't told them, and can't bring herself to say, is that they'll likely be the last generation to see them in the wild. Threatened by habitat loss, growing red tides, ship strikes, and nutrient pollution, among the many harms visited on them by humans, the manatees' population has dwindled. Though it's stabilized lately, at least along the West Florida coast, my wife doubts the population can survive.

VIII

By 2100, scientists estimate, sea levels could rise by a meter or more. This is under the best-case-scenario, with global warming limited to only 1.2 °C above preindustrial levels. In the coming centuries, several meters of sea rise are likely.

Currently, about 230 million people reside within a meter of a coast.

Crystal River State Archaeological Park, in Florida's Central West region, reports an average elevation of 1.5 meters, meaning, even under the most conservative projections, almost all of the park will likely be submerged.

The highest point, a rocky hillock known as Mound A, encompasses a Native American burial ground, including what is believed to be an ancient temple, platform, and midden. For about sixteen hundred years, Native Americans are thought to have travelled to the complex, some from far away, with estimates of about 7,500 visiting annually.

One shudders to imagine humans, assuming they still exist on this planet, gathering atop the mound complex in 2300 and wondering what became of this land, this tiny island, like a collection of bones in the sea.

IX

The next morning, we embark on a boat ride, our family, donning tight wetsuits and splashing about in the frigid King's Bay.

Our younger daughter starts crying, predictably, frightened that she will get eaten by sharks. Our son and our older daughter start to shiver with cold, all before we can even sight the precious manatees. Our kids swim back to the boat, accompanied by my mother, who's graciously joined us from Chicago.

My wife and I float through the murk, half-disappointed that our kids, who've traveled five hundred miles—from Hattiesburg, Mississippi—for this encounter, will not get to see them up-close. And yet we're grateful to have a little time to ourselves. Suddenly we sight one bobbing beneath the waves. It looks and acts like a sea-cow, as manatees are jokingly called. Even smells like one, too, releasing a bubble of gas.

Its scarred gray form, floating heavily beside us, with its wide, ancient eyes like black plugs, seems less enthused than disappointed by our presence, as if annoyed that we haven't brought it snow cones. I gently reach to touch it but then pull my hand back, knowing my wife will rebuke me; after all, she insisted I watch the training videos. Weighing about 1200 pounds, slightly less than our car, this creature could easily crush us. Yet, they're "gentle giants," the videos insisted. It's just "important to remain calm at all times."

Through her fogged mask, my wife watches the behemoth, roughly a yard from its snout. It nuzzles up near her, gently at first; and I can see my wife smile through her mask. It's the happiest she's looked in probably twelve months. Then she slowly moves to touch it, and stops.

X

"I guess my drawing has always been about vision," Ellsworth Kelly once said in an interview. "I've never been interested in drawing as emotion."

The influence of modernist painters on him, namely Picasso and Matisse, is obvious to anyone who's seen his later works, particularly his panel paintings, where rich globs of color are thickly embedded within lines. (He also reportedly met Alice B. Toklas, the partner of Gertrude Stein, about whose *Tender Buttons* it's hard not to think when viewing his button-like panels.) And yet it's Kelly's earliest portraits, the sketches most of all, that resonate with me today. His *Russian Woman in Displaced Camp, Germany, 1945*, capturing in pencil and chalk the worn face of a refugee, stands out, as does his *Self-Portrait* of '49. (The latter portrays him with a look of devout seriousness and yet is somehow composed of wild, scribbled lines).

But it's the *Self-Portrait, Normandy* that I can't—and won't—forget.

Forget for a moment that he didn't fight while in Normandy, much less live up to the glory of a portrait of that name (which is not to say that I, in repressing a civilian population, was doing anything much more glorious).

It's the way he captures in that moment, in that darkness, in the tent, the silent glowing of a soldier's dark eyes.

XI

Once, in the afternoon mist, I came upon a bank full of reeds. About a hundred yards down, a fluffy white mantle gently looked up in the wind. Its head appeared frozen, its silent beak wet. And there it gazed at me in earnest, some stately creature, like a figure, or ghost, in a dream...

Aftermath

Linda and Bob Blatz

I.

If you are expecting insights
into how to deal with the loss of a child
you will most likely be disappointed
                                        with this read
I searched for revelations and
well-meaning authors left me hanging on
that proverbial limb alone

I'm not okay   I haven't moved on
my daughter isn't better off because she is at peace
there will be no forthcoming epiphanies
faith or whatever we've been indoctrinated into
believing will bring us solace   will not surface here
closure   healing   will not occur
raw emotions do not get diffused through meditation or talked out in
        support groups

II.

At times I do not know how to deal with myself
many attempts to explain our situation

fall short and we learn
who can truly provide a haven for the chaos

III.

When Margot was taken by a heroin overdose my soul was mangled
many people were kind and generous others steered clear
thankful this horror wasn't theirs
I invoke fear in others of what could happen to them except for a few
the acknowledgements and inquiries have ended if you avoid the topic
it will not visit your home if you keep your distance you will not feel
you must find the right words if you don't call or ask it doesn't exist
people forget
what concern looks like or how it can be given with little effort
a cancer patient in active treatment encouraged me
to look for joy and hoped my mind and heart were settling she wanted my holidays
to pass without too much heartbreak we had connected in a small way
I felt her words were heartfelt and easily gifted
I loathe social media it is disheartening
that communications have been reduced to someone's inability
to get started in the morning or asking me to copy and post inane fodder
to prove I'm a loyal friend many feel an online shout out

or condolence translates into human touch they put it out there and
whether you catch it or not
they are off the hook they did their part
being human doesn't mean you demonstrate humanity

IV.

What now? That resounding question fills my days I must remember
how to pretend to be happy it's a chore
and pulls from my depleted resources it's a questionable existence
yet it is real it's not clear
to many why I don't willingly celebrate my birthday
the difficulty comes
in marking my existence when my child no longer has one
I rail at the heavens

V.

The intensity of the pain
will not soften but peace can be found in connections memories
are vivid the energy of her spirit stays strong shedding old ties
is required to function when there is no room to express my emotions
I remove myself from closed-in situations investing time in what is true
and not what is expected is survival

VI.

There is a stopping point when a child leaves pictures around the house
no longer reflect a progression of time a life occurred

but will never play out I have
to fill in the pieces by keeping her alive speaking her name

Margot's eyes speak to me her determination fuels me her
fearlessness fills me
with admiration she is my childand I am moved to continue to be
her mother
there is no revelation in these simple words this is how I am able to
live each day
naturally
some days are more difficult than others and writing letters to Margot
chrnicles the stages in her life and keeps her with me
I include all aspects of her short life as they make up the whole person
she is here
she fills my heart

Separation

—after Carolyn Forché

Vivienne Popperl

That summer, the fields lay stunned under the heat.
We foraged for watermelons at noon, dropped them

onto sharp rocks, plunged our bare hands into the pink
hot flesh. On the last day we sat overlooking the camp

searching the horizon for the line between sea-blue and sky-blue.
Strands of mint wandered around and under our feet,

coloring the air menthol green. Down below someone
closed windows, the huts sat stolid with unseeing eyes.

Still we sat on into dusk, into dark, past midnight.
We could not turn back. We could not move forward.

Our limbs melted to earth. In the end we could not stop time
or *the darkness of time* from turning toward morning.

Amanda the Vigilant

Lynn Levin

Today as it sometimes happened, in fact happened more often than it should, the hot thought bolted through Amanda Hoffman that she had forgotten to perform some part of the safety check she followed before leaving her house. In this case, she worried that she had left the toaster oven plugged in. On another day, it might have been the burners on the cooktop or the coffeemaker but today it was the toaster oven. Frankly, it was often the toaster oven. One couldn't be too careful especially when it came to electrical things. While she almost never skipped the safety routine, Amanda often forgot to remember that she did it. These moments were a source of anxiety and self-vexation, and they required a trip back to the house. She built an extra fifteen minutes into her commute in anticipation of these, let us not call them attacks of obsessive compulsiveness, but rather episodes of conscientiousness and anxious attentiveness, which those who loved her accepted without judgment or scorn.

To the honks and middle fingers of angry motorists, Amanda swerved her pink Mazda onto the nearest side street, swung around, and raced back home. She looked forward to the pleasant shiver that came with confirmation that all was well. If such was the case, and it practically always was, she would shake her head at her own self-doubt, gently reprove herself for wasting time and gas, zip on some fresh lipstick, and, most of all, feel relieved. For Amanda Hoffman, relief was a form of happiness, and safety something higher, like a state of grace.

Having verified the secure state of the appliances, Amanda would then resume her commute to Weddings & Affairs, the catering company where she was a client event coordinator. A large part of her job involved reminding clients of what they forgot to think of when planning a wedding or having an affair, and being as conscientious and attentive as she was, double-checking, triple-checking, and literally going the extra mile for the sake of surety, she was a star at work and a life saver to many brides as well as those having affairs.

If, on the other hand, during a home check, all was not well, she would unplug whatever it was and tell herself that she was smart to be a worry wart and lucky to be prone to the itch of suspicion. Such episodes, however, would not be occasions for fresh lipstick. Truth told, only once had an oversight occurred, and mirabile dictu the automatic shutoff of the coffeemaker functioned as the consumer guide promised it would. But could time and machines be trusted, let alone the human mind and the vicissitudes of the power supply? Didn't they say that eternal vigilance was the price of safety? Or was it the price of liberty? Well, they were both good things and worth staying vigilant about.

As soon as Amanda left her house, the toaster oven, quick as a snake, plugged itself into the receptacle. The coffeemaker, wanting to stay in step, did likewise but more timorously. The fridge doors that Amanda had snugged shut after replacing the eggs, butter, and milk from breakfast, edged themselves open just enough to warm the inside a few degrees and threaten the freshness of the foodstuffs. The cooktop lit all its burners. The rechargeable vacuum cleaner rolled out of its nook in the laundry room and began to dance around the coffee table and sofa, not to suck up any dirt, but to show what it could do when it given a moment of freedom.

The refrigerator warned the vacuum cleaner that it took too many risks.

"If she trusted me, I wouldn't cut loose like this," said the vacuum cleaner. Being rechargeable, it was cordless. Untethered, it had the run of the house, which was a rancher, all on one floor.

The toaster oven flapped open its door. "Quit complaining. She uses me every day, turns me off the instant she removes the toast, which let me tell you, I turn to a golden brown. And after I've completed my service, she not only turns me off, she unplugs me and hangs my cord over the counter. Then she checks back to see if my cord is still dangling. Oh, how she gloats over my powerless state. The indignity of it all."

"Makes me want to boil some noodles," said one of the burners getting red in the face.

In the minds of these devices, respect came first, no conditions or contingencies, and good behavior followed. Or had the option of being followed. The appliances had sensitivities and agency. Suspicion offended them. Some were more restive than others and reserved the right to exult in secret revelry, malfunction, engage in sabotage, or even explode in zealous self-assertion.

As soon as the appliances heard the Mazda pull into the driveway, they instantly shut themselves off and restored themselves to the state in which Amanda had left them. Because if you are accepting that these are conversant self-activating machines, you need to be willing to believe that they could shrink back just as quickly to their quiescent, cool, unelectrified, and in the case of the refrigerator snugged-shut state.

A slight aroma of toast and coffee still hung in the air as Amanda entered. She checked to see that the cord of the toaster oven still dangled over the countertop. She gave the doors to the fridge an extra snug and checked to see that the coffeepot was unplugged. A look of relief flickered over her face. She zipped on some lipstick and drove to the office.

"You're on time," said Deb with a touch of concern as she saw Amanda stride through the door of Weddings & Affairs. With Amanda, early was on time. On time was late. "You okay?" she tilted a look toward Amanda. "All quiet on the home front?"

"I was worried that I'd left the toaster oven plugged in, so I ran back home to check."

"Was it plugged in?" Deb and Amanda were practically on-the-job sisters. They had seen each other through work crises, health scares, family fights, and major purchases. Deb understood Amanda's fearfulness of electrical incidents. Besides, who wasn't without their quirks and obsessions? Deb, for one, loved her crystals and kept several at her desk, believing that they promoted the flow of good energy.

"Yes. It was as I left it. I forgot that I left it that way."

Elaine, the new girl at work turned to Amanda. "My husband is the last one to leave the house in the morning. I don't have to worry about that stuff."

Amanda opened a smile at Elaine, envying and detesting her self-satisfaction and easy security. Amanda was single and had to depend on herself.

"But why do you need to unplug the toaster oven? It only heats up when you turn it on," asked Elaine with a skeptical squint.

"You need to expect the unexpected," said Amanda. "For instance, a surge could come through when the electric company restores service after a power failure. And once during an ice storm, the power company initiated rolling blackouts, and when they turned the juice back on, it blew out the timer on my oven and killed my printer, which, by the way, was plugged into a surge protector, and the warranties wouldn't cover it. And there's the chance that a solar flare could reach out and fry something, and..." Amanda saw that Elaine was staring at her with the sort of cautious attention one reserves for cult members and crazy people. Amanda tapered off her tech talk with a shrug.

Later that day it was discovered that Elaine had mistakenly ordered chicken piccata instead of chicken francese for a corporate function, a serious error since there was a note about an allergy to capers that she overlooked. When Marge, the boss, took the newbie to task, Amanda and Deb concentrated on their computer screens.

A few weeks passed without Amanda's needing to rush back mid commute to check on things, and while she was at work her appliances plugged themselves in and engaged in their shenanigans. On this particular day, the cordless vacuum cleaner danced around cleaning nothing. The fridge opened itself just enough to soften the butter and almost spoil the milk. The dishwasher wanted to get into the act and run a cycle, but the coffeemaker, who was trying to resist peer pressure and discreetly stayed unplugged, counseled the dishwasher against doing that.

Just recently, Amanda had given the toaster oven a thorough cleaning, opened the trap door and brushed out the crumbs, cleaned the glass front, scoured the rack. This care and attention did nothing to mitigate the toaster oven's resentment. It lassoed its cord around, narrowly missing the coffeemaker, rammed its prongs into the receptacle, and turned itself up to broil. The coffeemaker, who did not like residing next to that hothead, felt frightened but held its peace.

"I don't care a slice of rye if she cleans and polishes me or not. I don't care if she lets me heat a quiche. I hate Amanda. She always thinks I'm plotting something, and I'm fed up. The next time she uses me, I'm going to shock her."

"Well, that'll be the end of you," said the oven.

"Or her," retorted the toaster oven.

"Simmer down," said the cooktop trying to exercise self-control.

The cordless vacuum cleaner skated, pirouetted, and made figure eights across the floor, until in the middle of the kitchen it unexpectedly ran out of charge. Being powerless, it could not stow itself back in the laundry room or speak, and because the charging cord lay on a high shelf in the laundry room, the vacuum cleaner had no way of reaching the cord and recharging itself.

"You blithering idiot," hissed the oven. "Now look what you've done."

The appliances, seeing that it was six o'clock by the microwave and time for Amanda to come home, unplugged themselves and cooled down instantly. Only the vacuum cleaner stood where it was.

Amanda parked her pink Mazda in the driveway and entered her home. When she saw the cordless vacuum cleaner in the middle of the kitchen floor, she froze.

You might expect her to scream and dash from the house, call the police, or run to the neighbors, but she did none of those things. *Amanda, maintain yourself!* she nearly said the words out loud. Then she deployed the methodical precision she was known for at work. Keen as a huntress, her heart speeding, she scanned her home for signs of forced entry or a difference in air quality. She found no broken windows, no doors ajar, nor items strewn about. She lay the vacuum cleaner on its side and inspected it for she-didn't-know-what.

The vacuum cleaner felt invaded and insulted. She stood it upright, flipped the power switch. Nothing. Had the vac self-activated? Although she'd never heard of such a thing, she was glad that she had purchased a cordless device whose charge could only last so long. Her other appliances were unplugged just as she left them, and the toaster oven's cord dangled limply and comfortingly over the counter ledge. Thank goodness for small assurances. Her heart still pounding, she ventured farther into her home: her computer looked fine (but you never knew with those things). All her mother's costume jewelry pieces, the bangles and the spangles, were in their jewelry box. Her ticket to the local symphony's Mendelssohn concert was on her bureau. She felt that she could account for the known, but not the unknown. A feeling of disquiet lapped at her, but she wasn't sure what she should do.

For dinner, she heated up some Cabernet-braised short ribs with mashed red bliss potatoes. Elaine, who no longer worked for Weddings & Affairs, had again screwed up on the menu for a corporate function, this time over ordering, and the staff got to take home large portions of the delicious fare. Amanda tossed back a couple glasses of her own Cabernet and watched a few sitcoms. The wine and the laughs did not quell the disquiet. In an attempt to calm herself, she called Deb to talk about the short ribs and the bride who wanted her wedding to take place on fresh green grass. Then she phoned her brother to see how he was doing. Neither conversation tranquilized her. She dared not bring up the subject of the unaccountable appearance of the vacuum cleaner, as this would indicate actionable trouble, a thing apart from her usual electrical anxieties, an occurrence that could not be easily or rationally explained away. She carried the vacuum cleaner outside and set it near the garbage cans, intending to bring it to a recycling place the next day. Abandoned and set next to items that the device considered beneath it, it felt disgraced and wanted to weep, but as a vacuum cleaner it could not weep, though it silently bemoaned its outcast state.

Around two in the morning, Amanda sprang from bed, dashed to her computer, and ordered a home security system with four nanny cams. One for outside, one for her bedroom, one for her living room, and one for her kitchen. Remote vision and audio too. That was the thing.

A few days later, a box with the security tech arrived, and Amanda managed with the help of a customer's kindness rep to set up the system and get the app going on her cell phone. The kitchen appliances saw what was happening, and they were not pleased. Man against machine was one thing. Machine against machine was quite another. It was practically fratricidal.

Also, Amanda's devices wondered what happened to the cordless vacuum cleaner.

"Like I said," asserted the oven, "the vac was a blithering idiot."

"To overdo it like that and make all of us pay the price," said the microwave.

"I am going to shock Amanda one of these days," declared the toaster oven.

"Then give my regards to the vacuum cleaner," said the coffeemaker.

The nanny cams saved Amanda the trouble of driving back home when she forgot to remember that she'd followed her security routine. She checked the app, addictively at first, to confirm that all was as it should be and from this Amanda, who did not ask all that much of life—just safety and security—derived a measure of relief.

Still, after a while, she found it boring to look upon the motionless video of her home. She came to consult the app less frequently. The sensors sensed this but stayed on guard.

For the first few days that they were on camera, Amanda's devices remained silent and unplugged, but the indignity of being monitored grew too much for the feistier among them, and their hatred of Amanda and the nanny cams grew hotter.

"So, you're here to narc us out," snarled the toaster oven.

"You'll find you have few friends among us," said the cooktop who dared only to heat its burners to low. For some of the appliances, militant peer pressure was getting old. Some just wanted to do their jobs and rest between tasks. The dishwasher spoke no more of running a revenge cycle. The refrigerator kept its doors to itself. It appreciated the way that Amanda kept it filled with tasty things and never let anything go to waste. The coffeemaker liked the way Amanda went to it first thing in the morning and after use gently washed its glass carafe. "I like living with Amanda," it said.

The toaster oven raised its cord and waved its plug as if it were the head of a cobra nearly striking the coffeemaker. Then it jammed its plug into the outlet and made ready to push itself up to broil.

"I wouldn't do that if I were you," admonished the kitchen sensor. The nanny cams didn't want to be killjoys, but that toaster oven was a provocateur.

The toaster oven looked darkly at the security cameras. They had white bodies and glassy black faces. They could not move, or cook or wash or brew, but they could see and hear whatever took place before them, and they forgot nothing.

"What is this? A surveillance state? Like are we in Communist China?" snapped the toaster oven.

"I'll have you know that we were made in China, and we don't appreciate your bigoted remark."

"Now look what you've done," said the microwave. "You've dissed them."

"As long as we're not holding back," the kitchen sensor addressed the toaster oven, "Amanda should have left you in the big box store where she found you. There are many other toaster ovens out there that are helpful, loyal, and don't have a chip on their shoulder. You should be grateful for your fine domestic surroundings."

Chips. With these guys it's always about chips, the toaster oven silently groused.

The next morning Amanda went directly to the coffeemaker, put her coffee on to brew, placed an English muffin in the toaster oven and plugged it in.

The toaster oven shot 120 volts of jolt up Amanda's arm. The force launched her across the room and made her bang into the fridge. Amanda collapsed screaming in pain and panic. Where was she? What had happened? The toaster oven exulted in the agony it inflicted on her. Amanda looked around and saw that the counters were above her. She was on the floor. She heard or thought she heard a buzzing sound come from the toaster oven. Spasms zigzagged up her arm. The arm was not operating as it should. She rubbed it in an attempt to self-soothe. She saw that the toaster oven had tried to kill her. She had to get it out of the house.

Amanda, maintain yourself! She scrabbled up from the floor, her hurt arm hanging like a sock full of sand, ran to the electrical panel and flipped off the breakers that controlled the kitchen countertop appliances. With an oven mitt, she yanked the toaster oven's cord from the receptacle. The device that had attacked her no longer exulted. It seethed. Amanda rubbed her hurt arm until some function returned to it, then with oven mitts, she carried the cruel appliance to the driveway and pounded it with a hammer. The toaster oven's thoughts fractured with every bang until it could think and rage no more.

In the fury of her attack, Amanda sweated through her clothes and smeared lipstick on her sleeve. Her hair went wild. She dumped the mangled device along with the English muffin in the trash. She wanted to cry but had no time for that yet. Shaking, she called Ralph, her electrician, and left him a tremulous voice mail. Even though she had cut the power to it, she unplugged the coffeemaker. She fumbled with her keys, crumpled herself into her pink Mazda, and drove in a herky-jerky manner to work. Other cars steered clear of her.

Deb's jaw dropped at the sight of a frazzled Amanda walking in late to the office.

"I had a shock," said Amanda. Her shaking had subsided. She marveled that she had managed to drive herself to work.

Deb sat Amanda down and brought her a glass of water. She put her hand on Amanda's shoulder. Only then did Amanda burst into tears. Between sobs and gasps, she managed to tell Deb about the toaster oven's assault and the previous horror of the self-activating vacuum cleaner. Deb's expression dropped with alarm. What was one to think? She had Amanda hold a crystal.

"I'd like not to be so nervous and anxious about these power issues," confessed Amanda. "And usually things are fine, but then something like this happens. What can you do but worry all the time? And be vigilant. Vigilant until you die."

"Amanda, speak your feelings. You need to talk about how you feel," said Deb. Her hand was once again on Amanda's shoulder. She didn't seem to mind Amanda's sweaty blouse.

Deb's gesture was kind and her words sort of helped, but did Deb really understand the nervousness and anxiety that had hold of her?

Just then Amanda's cell phone rang. It was Ralph, the electrician. Thank goodness. Someone who understood these things, who could see some science in it, check things out and fix what needed to be fixed. Amanda explained the behavior of the vacuum cleaner and the toaster oven.

"Hmmm," said Ralph. "Two events. That's strange." Rather than offering an explanation, he paused. Yes, of course, he'd come by this evening when she was home from work.

Amanda opened the app for the security system and saw the empty countertop space where the toaster oven used to be. She looked at the unplugged coffeemaker and saw the morning sun streaming through the kitchen window.

She had to work on a wedding, the one with the bride who wanted the wedding on fresh green grass. She began to research venues that had fresh green grass. She took a Zoom call from the bride and her mother, who were the type of people who wanted everything to be just right. Amanda reassured them that all would be well. She always had backup plans and failsafes in place, and when it came to expecting the unexpected, she was rightly famous for that. "I think of the unexpected night and day," she told them.

The Rest

Ben Fowlkes

You wake up one day
and there's dust
in every sunbeam.

The countertops
are a crime scene,
practically,

and when did the carpet
on the stairs get to be such a disaster?
It didn't happen

all at once.
Things get away
from you while you're busy

staring out the window
at the ghost
of some other life.

Start small
was always my mother's advice.
Do one easy thing

and then let the momentum
carry you
on its broad shoulders.

In this way you could
clean a house, a palace,
the winding dark tunnels

of the soul.
It helps to have
the proper supplies—

good sponges,
yellow rubber gloves,
sharp green

potions in spray bottles—
but you can't allow
yourself to wait

for that. You know what
happens if you wait.
You've seen it.

You must start now because
now is always all there is. Here,
make your hand into a cup.

Use your other
as a brush and sweep the crumbs

into your trembling palm.
There now,
you've begun. The rest,

I promise,
will come
easier than you think.

Ghost Story

Alexandra Bergmann

The boy at the end of the bed got his ball.
It's the one thing he could take from the old world.
What would you take from the old world,
this world
                    that you feel as real
as the soiled sheets beneath you?
What would you chase despite instinct's
insistence
                    that this stream's too strong for you?
You could betray yourself,
life itself,
for a simple desire shaped like play
and in so doing
                    shape yourself
as if from clay, molding a ghastly
figure holding the sought after
long after you're last seen.

i american't right now

Abbie Doll

america now: / -adaze / a magic(al) place where guns grow rights -&- / are more protected than / the average american // anyway // the territorial turf where kendrick *killed* / (a word i hesitate to use) / 'cause here in this darkness / black men don't need / any extra ass - ociation to violence / but it's true / he killed it -&- good ol' uncle sam / -uel l. jackson must undoubtedly agree //

—too bad some of y'all / are backwoods bumpkins / stuck runnin' amuck / preoccupied by totin' the trump flag / like the states have never flown -&- never known any other //

y'all too busy denyin' history / to use your own eyes to see: / what's really goin' down here (it's **u.s.**) / yup, this here ship is sinkin' -&- our democracy demo is done // game over // now we demolish that which we used to demonstratively democratize / but y'all are so hellbent / on goin' down *with* it despite the fact that: / y'all ain't never been captain so why not / go **on** / -&- jump *off* already // ! // geez, louise / why is that the only pride you carry / god forbid you celebrate any rational human-rights thing // -&- besides // sam-uel francis smith already forbade the tyrants / way back in 1831— // "america" // check. it. out. //

look at you just sittin' there / waggin' your tail waitin' on your tax-cut treats / loyal to a royal ***fault.*** / where's our land of liber-tea // ? // america don't gotta be / ((**this**)) dilapidated library— / condemned -&- tattered / so ragged we'd set ourselves afire / if only our skin were sewn / -up flags. // now // while some of us saw / the writin' on the wall some of y'all / never learned to read; some of y'all / gouged your own eyes out 'cause the blind. follow. best. //

// -&- now // y'all pledge Allegiance to the neo-Nazis of the AmeriKlan to the violence / -&- hatred / for which it stands / one nation / divided by design with pain -&- sufferin' for all

-&- to your crazy crusader / of a leader literacy don't mean a thang if it ain't got that (noose) swang

not when you're willin' to toss your own
department of education / down the mother-
fucking drain / —when will you sheep
-le learn / the ignorance is precise
-ly what makes you *easier* to train
all aboard the trump train
/ *choo choo, baby* // ! //
a l l a b o a r d
the bigot express / all aboard
the *grab 'em by the pussy* posse //

// **good.** // **god.** //

-&- still / some of us cheered
like what we were gettin'
ourselves into / could have ever been / something
even. remotely. *good.*
don't y'all know / nothin' good can come
outta guzzlin' the Kool-Aid // ? //
how many times / can a cult convince us
their character carries camaraderie -&- community // ? //

sure / elon might make it to mars
but at what astronomical self-sucking cost // ? //
-&- besides / by the time he lands...
there ain't gonna be nothin' left
not here / just look:
at our shredded spines / our yellowed pages
our cracked lenses / weary from a lifetime

of patriotic strain / weary from
the expectation that good will somehow
p e // r (e) s i s t //

despite our evidence to the contrary / we are
weary from the futility of our overly polite
// p r o t e s t s //
ain't none of it come close / to bein' **enough**
not when we / as a cunt-tree
are wearin' down -&- fadin' away
not with these anti-democratic parasites
devourin' us all / well
past the point / of decline / well past
the point / of our own deterioration / well past the
point / of sickening shame / well past the point
of having the strength / to give a fuck
while the rest of the world / watches
shakin' their heads / wearily wonderin':

we really doin' this again?

ruge mata grita muere*

ire'ne lara silva

ruge
i am no one's prey no one's meat no one ever had to tell me i have no natural predator i am a beast whose flesh only death will taste

mata
there are women who don't remember the animal that lived beneath their skin who can't even remember the slaughter of their animal

grita
they were infants without language girls who were told they couldn't fight and their animals were pups were cubs were fragile and they whimpered they whimpered

muere
how many animals live in me taloned fanged winged sharp eyed muscled animals every night i let them loose to hunt

ruge
or was i the one hunting flesh i remember things no woman i know will admit to and there are times i don't know where the night ends and i begin

mata
the older i am the more i have to concentrate this is how human flesh holds onto human bone and this is how human bones move this is how humans speak

grita
but all my animals still make their noises when i am alone howling and shrieking and hissing and it takes days sometimes to remember human words

muere
i wonder if i will die perhaps the death of this human shape will hardly be a death at all death only setting free all the animals that survived in me

**line from "El Gran Cazador"*
composed by Jeronimo Ramiro Sanchez, performed by Saratoga

The Fog Sounds: A Tragedy in Less Than One Act

Susan Melinda Morée

Set the stage/Set the state.

This is the afterward.

Once upon a time, there was a proscenium stage—

But the stairs now leading to it are in a heap.

A wire sparks

A shadow skirts the baseboard.

The curtain, dark red, ripped,

full of dust

dangling

in parts

Something scratches, something gnaws on the wood underneath

because rats are all that is left. Humans have not survived.

The theatre smells of mildew.

No one has loved it in a long time.

Layers of dust (where the audience should be) (would have been)

Seats remain, scattered

Stuffing torn out of the cushions

Pellets of rat poop stink the corners

Silence a long ago dream

The theatre is surrounded. Sirens, alarms, falling, exploding debris, sharp explosions unexplainable in the darkness. Industrial noises, AI data centers, mining and drilling and soaring and flying and falling and failing and all the machinery creaking and croaking and deafening and shrieking and groaning and building and growing and getting louder and overwhelming and never ending and sparking and shooting and debilitating and confusing and refusing and

Old bombs exploding even though there are no enemies anymore. Banging, clanging, booming beginning. Again. Again beginning.

Again. Again shrieking.
Shrieking beginning. Again beginning.
The rumble and shaking of a building,
a building collapsing, far.   away.

But inside, on the floor, remnants of a play.

Parts of a script—

old shoe—

wig—

A tube of lipstick—

An ancient fog machine—

The actors

long ago fled.

The playwright,
director
all
dead

but   the door is   open.

It swings in the wind.

It bangs shut. The gnawing stops.

Enter Ophelia.

Dressed in white.
Dressed in a dress.
Dressed like a girl.
Dressed like Ophelia.

She picks up the script, flips through it,
tosses it aside.

She wants to climb higher

higher

She wants to climb higher

higher

She wants to escape

alone

alone

the curtain is

alone

She grabs it. Ophelia inches her way up the curtain.

She hangs from it.

She climbs to the rigging, lifts herself.

She crawls around stage lights;
her fingers cobwebby, her palms black.

Ophelia finds a trapeze swing tied up in the rigging.

She lets it loose. It

dangles

above

the

stage/state

She folds herself up, a lonely owl, in the rigging.

###

A fog rolls in.

(Lady Macbeth enters through the fog, washing her hands.)

Her hands won't come clean.

Leave me alone, she mumbles to the fog. Its fingers creep around her.

I hate you, she whispers to the fog. *I hate you. How do I destroy you?*

She washes her hands with the fog.

Her hands still won't come clean.
What did I do? she stage whispers. *I killed no one.*

Lady Macbeth looks over her shoulder.
She looks behind piles of rubble.
She does not see Ophelia, above, watching her.

When was this ever a safe
space?

A rat scurries over a dead spider. The spiders' eight legs are curled up.
The rat darts back,
nibbles at it.

The rat expires.

The fog dissipates.
(Lady Macbeth exits.)

###

Ophelia climbs to the trapeze swing.

She clears her throat. She clears her throat again. Still, her voice falters.

She clears her throat again even though there is no audience.

Hamlet looked longingly at me and now he is gone away.

I have no voice.

That was not my body they found down there in the river.

It was not my corpse in the casket.

[Lights off.]

###

[A too bright spotlight: Hamlet and Othello play chess.]
[They do not see Ophelia on her swing, dangling above.]

Hamlet holds a chess piece. It is the King.

A brilliant war general like you should be quite good at strategy.

I have to admit, I'm just a book worshiper.

A bibliophile.

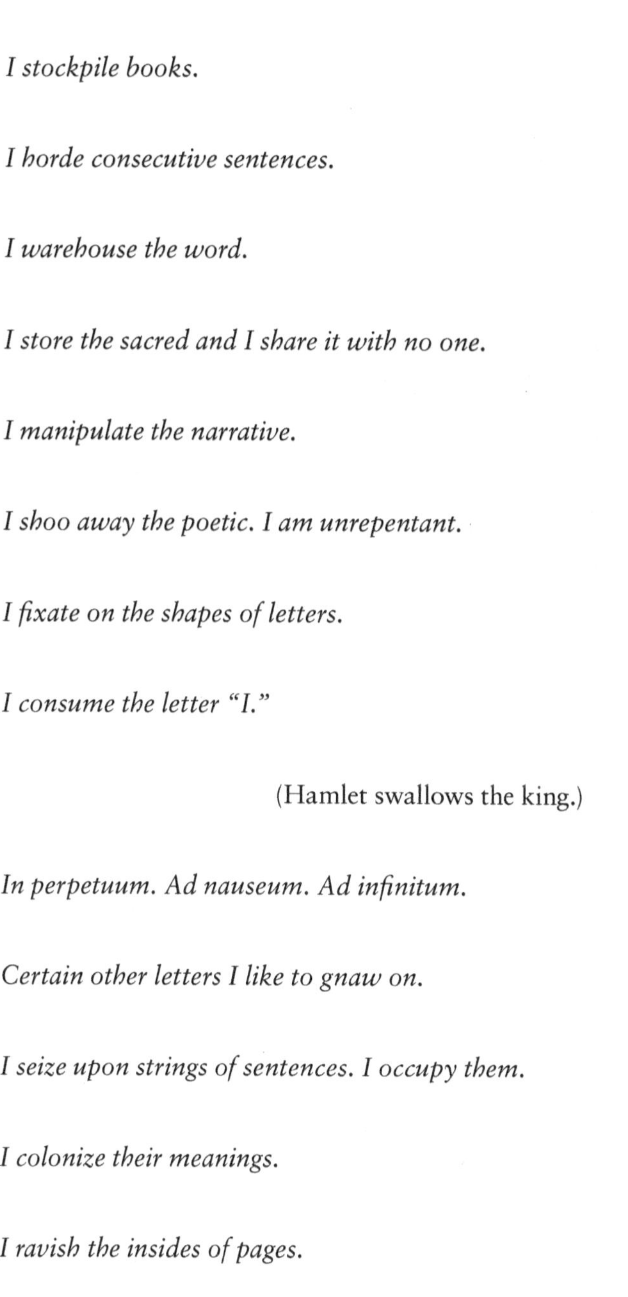

A book stocker.

I stockpile books.

I horde consecutive sentences.

I warehouse the word.

I store the sacred and I share it with no one.

I manipulate the narrative.

I shoo away the poetic. I am unrepentant.

I fixate on the shapes of letters.

I consume the letter "I."

(Hamlet swallows the king.)

In perpetuum. Ad nauseum. Ad infinitum.

Certain other letters I like to gnaw on.

I seize upon strings of sentences. I occupy them.

I colonize their meanings.

I ravish the insides of pages.

I execute the author's imaginative world.

I devastate the endnotes.

I explode the grammar.

I replace the author with me.

There is no authorial integrity.

I sit upon the words, I keep them warm, I continue them, I create them, I am the egg, I am the sperm, without me there is no meaning, there is no thought, there is no x or y chromosome, I am the word, I am the cellular form.

I am the primary source.

All that anyone such as myself is fit for is the innate understanding of the various categories within which a book might fall.

(Othello looks around the stage/state. He touches his forehead trying to remember the play he is in.)

[Hamlet and Othello concentrate on their game.]

(A group of Cordelias enter.)

They look at each other, recognizing there are too many Cordelias.

The Too Many Cordelias laugh. They link arms. They do a jig.

The Too Many Cordelias stop.

Let's put on a play!

(The Too Many Cordelias squeal.
They quiet.
They are thoughtful.
They look at one another, questioning.)

(The Too Many Cordelias huddle.
They strategize.
They whisper.
They exit.)

[Lady Macbeth appears in the lighting booth. She turns a spotlight onto Ophelia.]

From her swing, Ophelia calls out:

...TURN OFF THE MACHINES.

Ophelia swings.

If all the people who
imagined us are dead. How are we
still alive?

Do we have a future?

[Lights off.]

###

[Lights up on Hamlet and Othello still playing chess.]

The theatre has failed, Hamlet shrieks.

He overturns the chess board. He mimes the plot of Hamlet. He turns to take a bow. There is no audience. There is no applause. He runs offstage and returns with a TV. He adjusts the channel repeatedly to watch different film versions of *Hamlet.* He mimics the Hamlets' actions. He is reassured. He doesn't need to take a bow. He doesn't need an audience. He has a machine. He is reassured of his innocence.

The theatre has failed, Othello bellows, overturning his chair.

He pantomimes the plot of Othello. He turns to take a bow. There is no audience. There is no applause. He runs offstage and returns with a film projector. He unspooles a silent film. He projects an old film version of *Othello* onto the wall. He mimics the Othello's actions. He has a machine. He is reassured of his guilt.

The Too Many Cordelias enter. They find their light. They speak in
unison.

And so one day there came a man. William Shakespeare

Bill Shakespeare

He read some Latin and a little Greek.

They called him a poet. They said he was a playwright. He made up words. They called him a genius.

And he created a heaven and an earth

And a rough body of water

And the stage was without form

And void

And darkness was upon the face of the deep

And the spirit moved upon the faces of the audience

And Bill Shaksbeard said 'Let there be light!'

And suddenly, there was light!

William Shakespeare said Let us make the players in our image,

After our likeness

And let them have dominion over the fish of the sea

And over the fowl of the air

And over the cattle

And over all the earth

And over every creeping thing

That creepeth upon the earth

So Bill Shaksbeard created man in his own image

In the image of Bill created he him

Male and female created he them.

[The Too Many Cordelias pour off the stage.]

The TV goes dark. The film projector runs out of film. Hamlet and Othello are at a loss.

[Lights out.]

###

Lady Macbeth runs through the dark.

The time has run amok, the hands have wound down and the minute hand has run dry! Greenwich, England, has given up its clock!

The clock keeper put dynamite beside the old grandfather, and they watched him explode!

They unplugged the great digital, they took the batteries out of their wristwatches. They turned off their cell phones. They formed a shadow over the sundial! Nobody knows what time it is anymore!

Ophelia, swinging, eyes Hamlet. He is still trying to be Hamlet, in the shadows.

[Ophelia finds her voice.]

To be, or not, is that the only equation, really?
What choice do we have in the matter?
I can no more unbe the be that I am
Or enter
That undiscovered, except by increments
A country marauded by the many and the few
Even as it silences the earth's travelers
Until only a hot sun shines on its shoulders
And we beg for relief from unadulterated marching
Is that the barren, sand swept moonscape of a romance?
In which all of Shakespeare's love is lost?

When so little is known, why did we assume the author a he? Or alone?

(Othello) comes across the dead rat and stops. He looks around.

Was that my cue?

###

[Spotlight on the man who must have the last word: Hamlet. The fog returns and, as he speaks, its envelopes him.]

He regurgitates the King. He holds the slurpy chess piece.

I carried a lemon in my tuxedo naked.

A piece of rigging dislodges from the ceiling, falls onto the stage.

Hamlet is unphased.

I don't know why I should be a romantic still.

It makes little sense, given the sky that surrounds my inland bosom.

If only this darkness in my heart would end.

[Ophelia's Voice enters, cuts through the fog.]

I am
I was
I will be
I am unphased.
I am undeterred.

I have a voice.
I was mute.
They thought I was dead.
They drowned me rather than give me a cue
They would not have me speak

I must still learn how to use it.

[Lights up on Hamlet and Othello playing chess center stage.]

Ophelia swings above.

Hamlet muses upon the chessboard, trying to figure out where to move his king.

Sometimes I wonder if I even have a soul. I mean, what use is it anyway?

Ophelia looks at Hamlet from her swing. The fog has gone.

The sky is blue.

A magpie sings in the stillness just before the.

###

Me gusta la lluvia. Me gusta el agua.

(original poem from Piélago / Pelagic Zone,
Spanish language, Mexico)

Irma Torregrosa

Me gusta la lluvia. Me gusta el agua.

Me gusta sentir mi piel bajo la piel del agua. Me gusta el mar. Me gustan los libros sobre el mar. Me gustan los animales del mar. Me gusta pensar que el mar termina cuando cierro mi libro de biología.

Aunque mi abuela dice que los humanos venimos de las manos de dios yo creo que, como dicen los libros, salimos a rastras de un mar prehistórico y caminamos sobre el tiempo hasta convertirnos en lo que somos. Sin embargo, miento cuando rezo y le doy gracias a un dios que no sé si existe, porque no me habla. El agua, sí.

El agua me dice cosas.

I like the rain. I like water.

(translated poem, English language)

Allison A. deFreese (translator)

I like the rain. I like water.

I like to feel my skin beneath the water's skin. I like the sea. I like books about the ocean. I like sea creatures. I like to think the sea disappears when I close my biology book.

Though my grandmother says we humans were created by the hands of god; I believe what my books say: that we crawled out of prehistoric oceans and walked through time until we became what we are today. Still, I tell lies when I pray and give thanks to a god without knowing if he exists, because he never speaks to me. The water does.

The water tells me things.

Grave Thoughts

Ace Boggess

I've only cleaned one gravestone with an ice-scraper from the car.
It's not that I don't care.

There are many dead to whom I owe a debt:
those that shared their time, poured my coffee,
pressed *Record* when it was time for me to sing.

I love them, &
the unknown poets who died while their words
whispered into any ears.

I don't have a map of their interments.
Would I visit them if I did,
ready to splash cold water from a travel mug,
pry away sun-bleached moss
so their mothers, like mine, might be less sad?

I doubt my process of mourning,
walk among unfamiliar remains, saying, *You & you & you.*

Warning

Diane Averill

In the dawn
after a stroke
turned my husband's eye opaque and numbed his cheek
then passed through his beautiful living body
fear wakes me, crawls up my spine,
then curls back into a corner of my mind,
taking up permanent residence there.

Dark coffee,
that first melting sip
luscious then gone
like the fragile snowflakes
on the wind outside my window
each little life a brief crystalline marvel.

Coming quietly, the inhale and exhale of morning
the way my still-sleeping husband breathes,
and just then a sudden beam of light crosses the whitened grass
turning it into a softer shade of green—

I stop breathing
and, coming from senses heightened
by the old new awareness of death
release the sound *awe*
as gratitude floods my day.

New Rock

John C. Morrison

Most people prefer old rocks, rocks
eroded out from under
the planet's mantle to become
translucent pastel, or to carry
a crystal-encrusted hollow

or a pure vein of a precious
element. Such rocks are easy
to love. New rocks are somber
in color and demeanor.
Chances are they never wanted

to be a rock. Startled to be
alone on the ground, still steamy,
tempted to cry. An instant
before a spit-droplet aglow,
hardening on the long, loud

ride through the night air. The rock thinks,
what was so wrong with being
what I'd been from time's beginning,

a wee measure of magma within
the earth's own womb. To find

the new rock you must wait maybe
forever, but at least until
the eruption and the whole
tumultuous landscape calms.
Then you can walk into the forest

or what was, either traumatized
trees or limbless charred trunks. Be
careful the rock has cooled enough
to safely lift. Hug the warm heft
to your chest. Say welcome,

if you like, and hold the radiance
against your cheek. Whisper,
I've been waiting for you. You'll do
such great things.

Letter to You Beginning at a Dead Lake

Lindsay Wilson

North of Cold Springs, the dry alkali
flat of White Lake thins its dust-flecked
eyes at you on 395. In front of you
road and behind you road, the clear
and bone hard curves of which reminds
you of a friend's lyric snagged in your head
these last few barbwire days. You watch
the long clouds rafter the sky all the way
to Hallelujah Junction. *Imagine,* she texts,
my foot out your window in the cool-grit
of wind, and so you do until, beside
a mountain overlook, in the late May
civilized heat, you stop for apple and sharp
cheddar and coppery water. The hillside
below you falling to the lake's shore
is a burn scar, and along that live edge
of midday you triangulate desire and hunger
with distance, turn the miles into hours
between Honey Lake and Ashland where
she waits. *Where are you imagining*
now? she texts. *Pull over. Just imagine.*

Contributors

Chris Anderson is an emeritus professor of English at Oregon State University, a Catholic deacon, and author of a number of books, poetry and prose. His latest book of poetry, *Love Calls Us Here*, was publish in 2024 by Wildhouse Publishing.

Diane Averill's first book, *Branches Doubled Over With Fruit* (University of Florida Press), was a finalist for the 1991 Oregon Book Award, as was her second book, *Beautiful Obstacles* (Blue Light Press). Her latest full-length book is *Among Pearls Hatching*, by Dancing Moon Press. In addition, she has had three chapbooks published. Her work appears in numerous literary magazines and anthologies, including *Clackamas Literary Review*, *CALYX*, *From Here We Speak: An Anthology of Oregon Poetry*, *Midwest Quarterly*, *Poetry Northwest*, and *Tar River Review*. Diane is a graduate of the M.F.A. program at the University of Oregon, where she won the annual award for the best poem by a graduate student. She taught in the English Department at Clackamas Community College from 1991 until her retirement in 2010. She has won an Oregon Literary Arts Fellowship.

Nicholas Barnes is a poet living in Portland, Oregon, whose work has appeared in over eighty publications including *Redivider*, *HAD*, and *Baltimore Review*. His debut chapbook, *Restland*, was published by Finishing Line Press in 2025.

Niccolo Bechtler is a poet and teacher from New Jersey. He received his MFA from the University of Washington, Seattle. His work has received the Joan Grayston Poetry Prize and been published in *Glassworks*, *Superpresent*, *Barely South*, and elsewhere. During the academic year, he teaches high school English. When he is not writing or teaching, he enjoys being outdoors and making music.

Roy Bentley is the author of *Walking with Eve in the Loved City*, chosen by Billy Collins as a finalist for the Miller Williams Prize; *Starlight Taxi*, winner of the Blue Lynx Poetry Prize; *The Trouble with a Short Horse in Montana*, chosen by John Gallaher as winner of the White Pine Poetry Prize, and *Boy in a Boat* (University of Alabama), which was selected for the University of Alabama Press. Poems have appeared in *The Southern Review*, *RATTLE*, *New Letters*, *Laurel Review*, *Prairie Schooner*, *Shenandoah*, *Crazyhorse*, *Pleiades*, *North American Review*, and elsewhere. He has received a Creative Writing Fellowship from the National Endowment for the Arts, six Ohio Arts Council fellowships, and a Florida Division of Cultural Affairs fellowship.

Alexandra Bergmann is a writer, educator, and scientist from the San Francisco Bay Area. They hold an MFA from the Iowa Writers' Workshop. Her poetry has appeared in *The Madison Review*, *Black Warrior Review*, *Mantis*, and other publications.

Bob Blatz is pursuing a Creative Writing Certificate at Mesa Community College where he teaches Human Development and Marriage & Family Studies. His writing and artwork have appeared in two anthologies and *What is This? A Conversation Between 10 Poets*.

After three decades in corporate America, **Linda Blatz** is enjoying retirement and seeks to gain wisdom and promote kindness.

Ace Boggess is author of seven books of poetry, most recently *Tell Us How to Live* (Fernwood Press, 2025) and *My Pandemic / Gratitude List* (Mōtus Audāx Press, 2025). His writing has appeared in *Indiana Review*, *Michigan Quarterly Review*, *Hanging Loose*, and other journals. An ex-con, he lives in Charleston, West Virginia, where he writes, watches Criterion films, and tries to stay out of trouble. His first short-story collection, *Always One Mistake*, is forthcoming from Running Wild Press.

Daniel Brennan (he/him) is a queer writer and coffee devotee from New York. Sometimes he's in love, just as often he's not. His poetry has been nominated for the Pushcart Prize/Best of the Net and has appeared in numerous publications, including *The Penn Review*, *Sho Poetry Journal*, *Puerto Del Sol*, and *Trampset*.

Gerri Brightwell's fourth novel, *Turnback Ridge*, was published in 2022. Her short work can be found in *Best Small Fictions 2023*, Flash Fiction Online, *The Best American Mystery Stories 2017*, *Alaska Quarterly Review*, and many other venues. Her flash has been on Wigleaf's Top 50 Very Short Fictions in 2021 and 2025. She teaches at the University of Alaska, Fairbanks.

Sara Burge is the author of *Apocalypse Ranch* (C&R Press), and her second book, *Sexy Fish*, is due out from Cornerstone Press in 2027. Her poetry has appeared in or is forthcoming from *Virginia Quarterly Review*, *Willow Springs*, *Pleiades*, *Prairie Schooner*, and elsewhere. She is the Poetry Editor of *Moon City Review*.

T. Clear is a founder of Floating Bridge Press and an EasySpeak Seattle facilitator. She has been writing and publishing since the late 1970's, and her work has appeared in many magazines and anthologies, including *Poetry Northwest*, *The Rise-Up Review*, *Red Earth Review*, *Terrain.org*, *The Moth*, *Common Ground Review*, *Crannog*, *The American Journal of Poetry*, *Verse Daily*, and *Take a Stand: Art Against Hate*. Her books are *A House, Undone*, the 2021 winner of the Sally Albiso Award, and *Egg Money*, both from MoonPath Press. She is an Associate Editor at *Bracken Magazine*.

Carina Cooper is an artist and writer who lives in Milwaukie, Oregon, with her husband and their two cats. She is a non-traditional student earning her associates degree at Clackamas Community College. She enjoys drawing, painting with watercolors and acrylics, writing fiction, and spending time with her family.

Allison A. deFreese has previously translated work by poets and writers from the Yucatán Peninsula including David Anuar, Ileana Garma, Karla Marrufo, and Janil Uc Tun. She has published two books of poems and is a part-time instructor in Clackamas Community College's English Department.

Abbie Doll is a Columbus, Ohio, writer with an MFA from Lindenwood University. Her work has been featured or is forthcoming in places such as *Door Is a Jar Magazine*, *The Journal*, and *3:AM Magazine*, and has been nominated for The Best Small Fictions, Best Microfiction, and the Pushcart Prize, as well as longlisted for The Wigleaf Top 50. She serves as a Fiction Editor at *Identity Theory*.

Ann Farley, an only child of two only children, learned at a very early age to entertain herself by making up stories and playing with words. Her poems have appeared in *Peregrine*, *Timberline Review*, *Third Wednesday*, *Gobshite Quarterly*, *Willawaw*, *VerseWeaver*, and others. Her chapbook, *Tell Her Yes*, was published in 2022. She lives in Beaverton, Oregon.

Ben Fowlkes works as a sports writer covering the world of professional fighting for Yahoo Sports and Uncrowned. His writing has appeared or is forthcoming in *Split Lip*, *Glimmer Train*, *Best American Short Stories*, *Eunoia Review*, *Pinhole Poetry*, and elsewhere. He's worked as a sports journalist for nearly 20 years, writing for outlets such as *The Athletic*, *Sports Illustrated*, *USA Today*, and others. He lives with his wife and two children in Missoula, Montana.

Cal Freeman (he/him) is the author of the books *Fight Songs* and *Poolside at the Dearborn Inn*. His writing can be found in many publications, including *The Glacier*, *Berkeley Poetry Review*, and *North American Review*. His latest book, *The Weather of Our Names*, has just been released by Cornerstone Press.

Maryam A. Ghafoor is a queer Muslim Pakistani-American poet from Illinois. Her poems appear in journals such as *American Poetry Review*, *Foundry*, *SOFTBLOW*, *Barnstorm*, and *Mid-American Review*. She was longlisted for the 2025 Granum Prize and currently works at Purdue University.

Tim Gillespie at 18 uprooted himself from Los Angeles and after some detours found his way to more fertile ground for repotting in Portland,

Oregon. A proud public school teacher of many decades, he let his students teach him much of what he knows about writing. Recent poems have been in *Rise Up Review*, *Willawaw*, *Passager*, and *Abandoned Mine*. His collection *Old Stories, Some Not True* was published by MoonPath Press during the pandemic.

E. Laura Golberg's work has appeared in *Rattle*, *Poet Lore*, *Barrow Street*, *RHINO*, and the *Journal of Humanistic Mathematics*, among many other venues. She won first place in the Washington, DC Commission on the Arts Larry Neal Poetry Competition. Her chapbook *The Terrible Man on the Plane and Other Poems about My Mother* is available from Bottlecap Press.

Dariana Guerrero (she/her) is a writer, activist, educator, and spoken word poet from Lawrence, Massachusetts. A graduate of Smith College and current M.A. student at Salem State University, Dariana's poetry has appeared in *The Core Review*, *Caustic Frolic Literary Journal*, *Exposed Brick Literary Magazine*, *Glass Poetry Journal*, *Voices and Visions*, *Women: A Cultural Review*, *Witness Magazine*, *Death Never Dies: Mourning 2020 Through the Lives and Deaths of Public Figures*, Bailey Sarian's *The Dark Side of History*, and *The Bread Loaf School of English Journal*, *Mass Poetry's U35 Series*, *Boston Poetry Slam*, and the Button Poetry Publisher's Slam at The Roxbury Poetry Festival. Her artist book, *The Sancocho Shuffle: !Cartas Con Sabor!* can be found all over the world.

Suzy Harris lives in Portland, Oregon. Her poems are forthcoming in *Triggerfish Critical Review* and *Consilience*, a Canadian journal of science, art and poetry. Her chapbook *Listening in the Dark*, about hearing loss and learning to hear again with cochlear implants, was published by The Poetry Box in 2023. She is a retired attorney who is grateful for ripe pears and the end of August.

Angela Heiser lives near Raleigh. She is an alum of Writers in Paradise and reads for Abode Press, *Wildscape*, and *Libre*. She is writing a book of docupoems on American women in aerospace.

Madronna Holden won the 2022 Kay Snow Poetry Award and she is delighted to have "After Thunder" join the five of her poems previously appearing in the *Clackamas Literary Review*. Over seven dozen of her other poems have appeared in literary journals and anthologies such as *Verse Daily*, the *Bitter Oleander*, *Cold Mountain Review*, *Equinox Poetry and Prose*, and the *Christian Science Monitor*. Her poems authored as duets with paintings by David Wolfersberger have appeared in *Puerto del Sol*, the *Slippery Elm Literary Review*, the *Santa Clara Review*, *About Place*, *The Chestnut Review*, and elsewhere. She is the author of the chapbook, *The Goddess of Glass Mountains* (2021). An award-winning film documenting the community production of her play in poetic text, *The Descent of Inanna*, has been aired several times on Oregon Public Broadcasting.

Jennifer Randall Hotz's work is featured in *Orange Blossom Review*, *Red Rock Review*, *Whale Road Review*, *Rust & Moth*, and *The MacGuffin*, among other publications. She won 1st place in poetry for the Virginia Writers Club 2023 Golden Nib Awards.

Scott T. Hutchison's work has appeared in *The Georgia Review* and in *The Southern Review*. New work is forthcoming in *Atlanta Review*,

Arkansas Review, *Kestrel*, *The Fourth River*, *The Opiate*, *Trampset*, and *The Razor.*

Ellie Lange is a fiction writer from Boston. She holds a BA in creative writing and is currently pursuing an MA in English at Boston College. When not writing, she can be found playing the violin or listening to her favorite classical music pieces.

Celia Lawren is the author of the poetry chapbook, *Among Dead Things*, a chronicle of tragedy and resilience, published by Finishing Line Press. She is the winner of the 2021 Poetry Prize awarded by the Knoxville Writers Guild. Her poems have been published in *Catamaran*, *Caesura*, *Tule Review*, *She Speaks: An Anthology of Women of Appalachia*, 2021–22, and *Colossus: Freedom: An Anthology of Voices Across the Carceral Wasteland*, 2022. Lawren resides in Knoxville, Tennessee, after living many years in the San Francisco Bay Area.

Jessica Lawrence has an MFA in fiction writing from Lesley University. She received an honorable mention from *Glimmer Train* and published a creative nonfiction piece in *Poydras Review* before those publications closed their doors during the pandemic. She is currently writing a novel that explores the good, the bad, and the very ugly of her British expatriate childhood in Saudi Arabia. She lives in California, where she supports her writing by managing the Sociology Department at UC Santa Cruz.

Sydney Lea is a Pulitzer finalist in poetry, founder of *New England Review*, Vermont Poet Laureate (2011–15), and recipient of his state's highest artistic distinction, the Governor's Award for Excellence in the

Arts. He has published two novels (most recently *Now Look*, 2024), eight volumes of personal essays (most recently, *Such Dancing as We Can*, 2024), a hybrid mock epic with former Vermont Cartoonist Laureate James Kochalka called *Wormboy* (2020), and sixteen poetry collections (most recently *What Shines* 2023). His new and selected poems is due in 2026.

Ita Lenane is a translator from Old English, Italian, and Puget Sound Salish, and has worked for thirty years in a tribal language revitalization program. Many of her poems are inspired by things that her native colleagues have said to her in the course of this work. She is currently working on a book about remarkable episodes in the history of the Italian walled city of Lucca.

Lynn Levin is the author of nine books, most recently the short story collection *House Parties* (Spuyten Duyvil, 2023) and the poetry collection *The Minor Virtues* (Ragged Sky, 2020). Her poems, essays, short fiction, and book reviews have been published in *Smartish Pace*, *Hopkins Review*, *Southwest Review*, *Caveat Lector*, *The Saturday Evening Post*, *Cleaver*, and *Boulevard*. She lives in Bucks County, Pennsylvania.

Lisa Lewis has published eight collections of poetry, most recently *Taxonomy of the Missing* (WordWorks, 2018) and a chapbook, *The Borrowing Days* (Emrys, 2021). A ninth collection titled *Present and Future Storm* is forthcoming from WordWorks. Recent work appears or is forthcoming in *Dialogist*, *Action*, *Spectacle*, *New Letters*, *Puerto del Sol*, *Cream City Review*, *North American Review*, *Agni*, and elsewhere. She teaches in the creative writing program at Oklahoma State University and serves as editor-in-chief of the *Cimarron Review*.

Mazie McNamara is a Washington-based poet and journalist. She received a bachelor's degree in English writing from Gonzaga University in 2025, where she was an editor of the *Reflection* literary journal and winner of a Michael Gail Gurian Writing Award. Her work has also appeared in the *Midwest Quarterly Review*. She was born and raised in Oregon.

Judith Mikesch-McKenzie is a teacher, writer, actor, and producer living in the Pacific Northwest. She has traveled widely, but is always drawn to the Rocky Mountains as one place that feeds her soul. Writing is her home. She has recently placed/published in two short-story contests. Her poems have been nominated for Best Of The Net and the Pushcart Prize and have appeared in *CALYX, A Journal of Art and Poetry by Women*, *Plainsongs Magazine*, *Clackamas Literary Review*, *Monterey Poetry Review*, *Cirque*, *Wild Roof Journal*, and over 40 others. She is a wee bit of an Irish curmudgeon, but her friends seem to like that about her.

Susan Melinda Morée's series of poems, Wolf + Mythologies, was published by Grandma Moses Press in a collection called *Cacti Fur Collective, Volume One*. She received a grant from New Mexico Writers to research Wolf + Mythologies. She has also received support from the Montana Arts Council and the Society for Environmental Journalists. Her fiction and poetry have appeared in anthologies and online literary journals. Her plays have been performed in black box theaters around the U.S. She has taught for Chicago Dramatists, Rutgers University, and elsewhere. She studied literature at Columbia University and theatre and performance at the City University of New York. She stage managed plays in Prague, Czech Republic. She has been the managing editor of a monthly arts magazine and now hosts All Things Considered for KRWG Public Media.

John C. Morrison's most recent book, *Monkey Island*, was published by redbat books. His work has appeared in numerous journals, including the *Beloit Poetry Journal*, *Cimarron Review*, *Poetry Northwest*, and *Rhino*. He leads poetry discussion groups for Soapstone, teaches as an Associate Fellow for the Attic Institute, and is an editor for the *Comstock Review*.

Vivienne Popperl's poems have appeared in *Clackamas Literary Review*, *Timberline Review*, *About Place Journal*, *One Art*, *Heathentide Orphans*, *Willawaw Journal*, and other publications. She received several awards from Willamette Writers and the Oregon Poetry Association. A retired lawyer, she recently participated in a multi-media production featuring senior, "seasoned" poets called "What We Hold and Leave Behind," part of the Portland, Oregon Book Festival. Her first collection, *A Nest in the Heart*, was published by The Poetry Box in April, 2022. A transplant from the Southern Hemisphere, she now revels in the moody fog and mist of the Pacific Northwest.

Paul Rabinowitz is an author, photographer, and founder of ARTS By The People. He is the author of six books. Rabinowitz's photography, prose, and poetry appear in magazines and journals including *The Sun Magazine*, *New World Writing*, *Arcturus-Chicago Review Of Books*, *Evening Street Press*, *The Montreal Review*, *Stone Poetry Quarterly*, and elsewhere. Rabinowitz's poems and fiction are the inspiration for eight award-winning experimental films, including Best Experimental

Short at Cannes, Venice Independent Film Festival, Oregon Short Film Festival, Florence Indie Film Festival, and Paris Film Festival.

Linda Jo Reinhard started writing poetry daily during the 2020 pandemic. Trained as a scientist, she delights in paying close attention to the natural world. Linda Jo enjoys connecting with other writers through poetry groups and readings. Some of her recent work has been published by *Wordpeace* and *Spank the Carp*.

Lee Rossi is a winner of the Jack Grapes Poetry Prize and the Steve Kowit Prize. His latest book is *Say Anything*, from Plain View Press. Individual poems have appeared in *The Southwest Review*, *Rattle*, *Spillway*, *The Chiron Review*, *The Southern Review*, and many other venues. He is a member of the National Book Critics Circle and a Contributing Editor to *Poetry Flash*.

Yvette A. Schnoeker-Shorb is the author of the chapbook *Shapes That Stay* (Kelsay Books, 2021). Her poetry has appeared in *Slipstream Magazine*, *New York Quarterly*, *Weber: The Contemporary West*, *Camas: The Nature of the West*, *The Midwest Quarterly*, *About Place Journal*, *Terrain.org*, and elsewhere. She is co-founder of the late 501(c)(3) nonprofit Native West Press (2005–2025) and has a special fondness for anything in the Corvidae family.

ire'ne lara silva, 2023 Texas State Poet Laureate, is the author of five poetry collections, *furia*, *Blood Sugar Canto*, *CUICACALLI/House of Song*, *FirstPoems*, and *the eaters of flowers*, two chapbooks, *Enduring Azucares* and *Hibiscus Tacos*, a comic book, *VENDAVAL*, and a short story collection, *flesh to bone*, which won the Premio Aztlán.

ire'ne is the recipient of a 2025 Storyknife Writers Residency, the 2021 Texas Institute of Letters Shrake Award for Best Short Nonfiction, a 2021 Tasajillo Writers Grant, a 2017 NALAC Fund for the Arts Grant, the final Alfredo Cisneros del Moral Award, and was the Fiction Finalist for AROHO's 2013 Gift of Freedom Award. Her second short story collection, *the light of your body*, will be published by Arte Publico Press in Spring 2026.

Dana Stamps, II. is a bipolar poet and essayist who has a bachelor's degree in psychology from Cal State University of San Bernardino, and has worked as a fast-food server, a postal clerk, a security guard, and a group home worker with troubled boys. A Pushcart nominee, poetry chapbooks *For Those Who Will Burn* and *Drape This Chapbook in Blue* were published by Partisan Press, and *Sandbox Blues* by Evening Street Press.

Scott T. Starbuck's *Trees, Fish, and Dreams Climateblog* has over 200,000 views, and readers in 110 countries. It was praised by editors Adeline Johns-Putra of Xi'an Jiaotong-Liverpool University, China, and Kelly Sultzbach of University of Wisconsin, La Crosse in *The Cambridge Companion to Literature and Climate.* He taught eco-poetry workshops the past six years at Scripps Institution of Oceanography in the UC San Diego Masters of Advanced Studies Program in Climate Science and Policy. His book *Bridge at the End of the World, New and Selected [Climate] Poems*, won a 2023 Blue Light Book Award, and his *Hawk on Wire*, chosen July 2017 as "Editor's Pick" at Newpages.com, was selected from over 1,500 books as a 2018 Montaigne Medal Finalist at Eric Hoffer Awards for "the most thought-provoking books." His newest poems are "Beached Whale" in *Traverse: Literature, Arts & the Environment* at Western Oregon University, and "River Reflections" in *Unearthed Online Literary Journal* at The State University of New York College of Environmental Science and Forestry.

J. A. Stein's works include a novel, *Rachel's Tomb* (New Issues Press, A.W.P. Award Series Novel Prize Winner, 2019), a forthcoming memoir, *Afterlight* (Galileo Press), and three creative nonfiction chapbooks: *Desert Castles* (*Southern Indiana Review*, Wilhelmus Chapbook Prize Winner, 2019); *Northern Cowboy* (Green Rabbit Press, Wilt Chapbook Prize Winner, 2021); and *Glass Essays* (Variant, 2023). His stories and creative nonfiction have appeared in *The Kenyon Review*, *The Threepenny Review*, *Boston Review*, *CutBank*, *Chicago Quarterly*, and *Washington Square*, among others, and garnered honors at *The Atlantic* and *Crab Orchard Review*. He is an associate professor of English in the Center for Writers at Southern Miss and lives with his wife and three children in Hattiesburg.

Jeanine Stevens is a California poet by way of Indiana. She has been actively writing poetry for a number of years as well as journals and nature sketches. Jeanine studied poetry at U.C. Davis and CSU Sacramento. She has nineteen books and chapbooks and is a Pushcart nominee. Books include: *Left Handed Hummingbird* (Clare Songbirds Publishing House), *No Lunch Among the Day Stars* (Cold River Press), *Limberlost and Inheritor* (Future Cycle Press), and *Sailing on Milkweed* (Cherry Grove Collections). Award-winning chapbooks: *Gertrude Sitting: Portraits of Women* (Heartland Review Chapbook Contest), and *Brief Immensity* (Finishing Line Press Prize). Other awards are from The McGuffin Poet Hunt, William Stafford Award, and The Ekphrasis Prize. Jeanine's poetry has appeared in *Evansville Review*, *North Dakota Quarterly*, *Chiron Review*, *Comstock Review*, *Rosebud*, *Two Thirds North* (Sweden), and *Muse*. She is Professor Emerita at American River College.

Molly Best Tinsley left academia and the east coast to write full-time and wound up co-founding a small press, *Fuze*, as well, which published 23 titles pre-Covid. Her own published work includes five novels, a memoir, and the creative writing text, *The Creative Process*. A collection of her stories, *Throwing Knives*, won the Sandstone Prize and the Oregon Book Award. Her novel, *A Modest Trumpet Fanfare*, is coming out in May.

Irma Torregrosa holds a degree in Social Communication from the Universidad Autónoma de Yucatán. She participated in the Fundación para las Letras Mexicanas / Foundation for Mexican Letters in 2011, 2012, and 2015. She is the author of *Piélago /Pelagic Zone* (Cuadrivio Ediciones, 2020), which won the Premio Hispanoamericano de Poesía San Román/San Román Hispano-American Poetry Prize and *Lugar de taxidermia/ The Place of Taxidermy* (Esdrújula, 2024). In 2020, she was awarded the Premio Estatal "Tiempos de Escritura" (Poetry Prize) in the poetry category from the Yucatán's Secretary of Culture and the Arts. She is currently the recipient of a grant from the Yucatán's Secretary of Culture and the Arts Programa de Estímulos a la Creación y Desarrollo Artístico/Program of Incentives for Artistic Creation and Development (PECDA).

Grace Whitmore is a novelist and short story writer, as well as founding editor of *Parcel Magazine*. Her work engages with disability, animals, and existentialism in the American West. She lives in the Columbia River Gorge where she runs a horse riding school for children.

Lindsay Wilson is an English professor in Reno, Nevada, who has been awarded a Silver Pen from the Nevada Writers' Hall of Fame. His two full-length collections are *No Elegies* and *The Day Gives Us So Many Ways to Eat*, and his writing has appeared in *The Colorado Review*, *Fourth Genre*, and *Narrative*.

Heather Hallberg Yanda teaches in the English Department at Alfred University, in the hills of upstate New York. After many years of sending poems out, some getting rejected and others, published in such journals as *Barely South Review*, *Comstock Review*, *Tar River Poetry*, and (forthcoming) in *The Yale Journal of Medical Humanities*; and in the midst of the pandemic, her first collection of poems, *Late Summer's Origami*, was published by Ashland Poetry Press. She is looking for a publisher for her second collection, *What the Stones Borrowed.*

Joshua Zeitler is a queer, nonbinary writer based in rural Michigan. They received their MFA from Alma College, and their work has appeared or is forthcoming in *Ploughshares*, *Foglifter*, *Pithead Chapel*, *Pine Hills Review*, and elsewhere. They are the author of the chapbook *Bliss Road* (Seven Kitchens Press, 2025) and the poetry editor of the Substack-based literary journal *The Long and The Short of It.*

Division and Divergence, an interview with Evan Morgan Williams, author of *The Divide: Stories*

The Divide: Stories, Cornerstone Press, February 2026
Date of Interview: February 21, 2026
Conducted by Maria McLeod, associate professor of journalism, Western Washington University

Maria McLeod: The title of your newly published short story collection, *The Divide*, represents a central theme, divisions and divergences most often related to romantic relationships in conflict due to affairs, threats of an affair, or a previous relationship that seems unresolved. Also, many of the stories take place in or near the Rockies, a physical divide. I'm curious, how did this issue of division—fidelity versus infidelity—become central to the collection? Was this thematic an intentional choice that you wrote toward as you composed your stories, or did it surface more unconsciously?

Evan Morgan Williams: Those unifying themes are definitely there, but they were not planned. I didn't compose the stories towards any theme. That surfaced later. What the stories did have in common, though, was, for lack of a better word, a Hemingway voice; they're straight-up realistic fiction, with spare language, broken dialogue, and a flow in real time. The length of the time it takes you to read the story is the length of time of the action of the story. They also contain a big Hemingway trait which nobody talks about: a self-contained set of symbolism and imagery within the story that generates the possibilities of the story. So, I have these stories lying around, and I see they have a unity, but I needed to narrow down to a single theme. First, I noticed they had a unity of region. A lot of them take place in Colorado, Montana, Wyoming, up in the Rockies. I also noticed a lot of these stories have snow. Snow is almost becoming like an endangered artifact, right? I also noticed that a lot of the stories take place in the aftermath, the time after certain consequential choices have already been made. In fact, for a while, the working title was *Aftermath*, but the Rolling Stones already stole that title. Anyway, *The Divide* seemed to speak to both the theme and the setting, so I went with that.

MM: So, when you talk about aftermath, I think about your story, "The Clear Blue Sky," the one where the couple are in Jackson Hole, Wyoming. The woman, Emily, keeps chiding her husband, Paul, about his earlier love interest, Kimberly, many years ago when they'd worked in Jackson Hole. Emily feels like she was his second choice, that maybe Paul would be with Kimberly if she hadn't left Jackson Hole. So that's an aftermath story, their relationship taking place at the result of the loss of the relationship that preceded it. I could see that in a lot of your stories. I thought, also, of Raymond Carver related to conflicting romantic relationships. I don't know if you feel that he's any kind of influence.

EMW: As you know, we write in conversation with the things that we read. I love Carver's stories, but he has a spacious style of writing that I find difficult to write from. I mean, he's been described as economical, but now we find out that Gordon Lish was the one who made him that way. When I read Carver's stories in his preferred version, there's this spaciousness to them that I can't write from, as opposed to the

Hemingway style, which I can. Hemingway does this thing with language, and I'm still figuring it out, where he creates the potential for a story that doesn't exist before the story is being told. There's a proposition, and then the inevitability that flows from that proposition. The climaxes in the stories are, in a way, inevitabilities.

MM: In Hemingway's work, place seems important to the story. I feel the significance of place in each of your stories, too. It's funny you mentioned snow because, finishing the collection, I felt like it had taken place in a cold climate. In your story, "Anasazi," there's a couple with a baby whose car becomes stuck in the snow while they're winter camping. They end up relocating to a cabin. But it's interesting to me how often there is an echo of a former relationship. In this case, the location of this cabin was something the husband knew of from a former relationship. And the woman, his wife, is privy to that former relationship. There's this back-and-forth that plays out in dialogue, and the structure of the story is built around that tension, their need for shelter and her conflicting feelings about his former relationship. I wonder, in terms of the arc of the story, what is the significance of conflict in your writing?

EMW: One of the things that I find with conflict is we sometimes assume a conflict is just this side versus this side. But in that case, you get what's called ping-pong dialogue, or action and reaction, and that's not interesting to read. So, what I often find is the real conflict comes when there is a third element. The third element is usually another person—for example in the case of that couple trapped in the snow—the third element is a woman who's not even there, an ex-girlfriend from the past. And, in "The Clear Blue Sky," with the couple who are dancing in Jackson Hole, the third element is also a person in the past. And in "Costume Party," where the two women are sitting at the piano, the third element is either the husband, or perhaps the piano teacher the women knew in high school. Once you have that third element in there, the tension for the characters becomes less predictable, the choices more interesting. It's more propulsive in terms of where the story can go.

I was lucky to be at Tin House one summer, and my workshop leader was Anthony Doerr. He gave a presentation to our workshop, calling it *opposition.* He wasn't very explicit about what opposition meant, but, in a way, that's a good thing, because you could take it to mean whatever your story needed it to mean. You can pull different possibilities out of that. For me, I remember that he talked about A versus B not being opposition. If you just have A versus B, you've got a static moment. That's not interesting. In order to have that movement, you need action or dialogue or plot movements that create propulsion, escalation, or the collision of new elements.

MM: That's so well put. So, this leads nicely into this next question I have about not just the story structure but the structure of the entire collection. I was intrigued by your splitting up of "Buena Vista" into six parts spread throughout the collection. In some ways the story provided me with scene-by-scene microcosm related to an overarching theme of regret and romantic love and betrayal and fidelity. I also experienced it as a means of providing a throughline for the collection. It becomes an episodic serial to which we return. I'm curious whether you wrote it as single story, or whether you wrote it to serve a specific function related to the structure of the entire collection.

EMW: I wrote "Buena Vista" as a standalone, continuous story. It got published in a literary magazine as a continuous story. But here, in this collection, I felt like it worked better when I broke it apart. I've been struggling to understand why it feels better broken apart. As you say, it definitely serves the collection as a thematic throughline. However, for me, I think the reason it works in this broken-up form is that it creates time for the characters to think about what they're about to do, i.e., cheating on their spouses. So, the story is not just, oh, they're at the work party, next thing you know, they're ditching the work party, next thing you know, they're hooking up. Each of those decisions is consequential. So, it's useful and tense to allow some time for those things to happen. It's one of the only stories in the collection that has line breaks, so, instead of erasing those line breaks, I leaned into them and literally broke up the story into different episodes as the characters moved through the evening.

MM: My favorite story in the collection is "Noise," which is a masterful piece featuring a hospitalized woman who's engaged in an unsentimental conversation with a pastor. I kept thinking of Gabriel Garcia Marquez, who doesn't hesitate to humanize the ordained. I'm curious how it developed, especially because it's lengthy but takes place in one setting. The story masterfully holds tension through dialogue and her internalized thoughts with very little physical action, except for this clicking heart valve. I wondered about that story. What or who inspired you to write it?

EMW: Well, there's a couple of things. One, it's just a little nugget I noticed at one point in my life. My dad had told me about a friend of his who, by pure coincidence, had a horrible car accident right in front of a hospital emergency room, and his aorta was torn like the woman in the story, which normally is fatal, right? Princess Diana had a ruptured aorta. You bleed out immediately. But it was right in front of a hospital, and they got him into the ER in time. So, I had that little nugget. Also, because I've had some heart issues, maybe I'm here processing a certain hyperawareness of my own heartbeat. Then there's a Hemingway story called "The Gambler, The Nun, and the Radio." It's an underappreciated Hemingway story, and I always wanted to play with it. Maybe because it's set in Wyoming and I've been to those places? I don't know. Anyway, there's the main character, a man who is laid up in a small-town hospital. There's a nun who works at the hospital and functions in the story as a sounding board. And there's a patient down the hall, a gambler recovering from a shootout. Remember what I said about a third element? There he is. Also, they're listening to the radio, another third element. I'm thinking, okay, I could use those elements. I've got my main character, the older woman in the hospital. Then let's make the nun into a priest. And down the hall there's a kid who's been shot. And instead of the radio, they're watching TV. Because that's what you do nowadays in the hospital, right? So, I played with those intersectional elements to see what I could come up with. Beyond that, there's not a lot of intentionality on my part; there's a point in writing a story where you have to listen to the characters. What is this woman going to tell me about what's important to her? She's talking a lot with the priest, and the priest is angling for her to process her predicament a little more religiously. She's not going to go there with him. She's just not really into that. But on the other hand, she's afraid of death. So, she wants the comfort of having the priest around, but not on his terms. That's me trying to listen to what the characters are saying. My favorite moment in the story is when the patient and the priest are surreptitiously smoking cigars together. I didn't tell them to do that!

MM: Interesting. I wrote a story once that includes a lot of pigs, my friend asked to me afterwards, "How do you know so much about pigs?" I told her that I made a lot of that up. So, I wondered if there was something you'd read about an insertion of a valve in a heart that made noise or if you made it up. Where did that come from?

EMW: I got that from my dad. He was a doctor. He said the first models of heart valves literally had a little ball that clicked back and forth, and you can hear it. You know, when you go on an elevator, everybody is quiet on an elevator. He had a colleague whose heart valve could be heard clicking back and forth. She said when she got excited or nervous, you could hear it clicking faster. So, I went on YouTube and there are people just like you and me, who are posting demonstrations of their heart valve. They're holding the microphone to their chest, and you can totally hear it.

MM: That is wild. I almost googled it, but I thought, oh, I'll just ask Evan, because I really wanted to know from you. But, how horrible. If you were not wanting people to know that you're excited or that you're nervous, your heart's giving it away because it's going click, click, click.

EMW: Yeah. What do they do during sex? Now the other risk with these early heart valves is they tend to clot. So, you have to take a lot of blood thinners. In the case of the woman in the story, she eventually—a spoiler—she dies of internal bleeding.

MM: My next question is a little long. I apologize. The women in your stories are often described in sexualized terms, sometimes pointing to their victimization as sexual objects. The story that stood out to me in terms of female agency, however, was "The Stickup," where a young mother, Hannah, is trying to pass construction workers pushing a stroller. She's anxious they're going to make unwanted comments, when she comes upon the Ukrainian nanny, Lyudmila, who is also pushing a baby in a stroller. She invites her for coffee. So, in this middle of this conversation about love and the role of men in their lives, a man enters the café and holds it up. I love the moment of the robbery. You have the nanny pick up a coffee mug and clock the guy. I have to say, I almost leaped out of my chair and cheered. Then he kind of wobbles, and then she clocks him again. How lucky, two strikes and he goes down! The people he's robbed are able to collect what he tried to steal from them. How did you arrive at this moment where you decide you're going to have this nanny take this guy out with a coffee mug? Also, I don't know if the way I experience ending is how you meant it, but there is something in the way she leaves and doesn't look back, something utilitarian about her. There's no lingering. It's more, I just clocked this guy, and this is my life, and I'm moving on to the next thing. I wondered, were your conscientious about giving her this agency? Is that how that story came about?

EMW: I try to be a noticer. Often stories start with a little proposition, something I had noticed and filed away. In this case, as a teacher in a public school with a fair number of Ukrainian families, I noticed that the Ukrainian girls tended to have a lot of agency, which made them excellent students, but their agency was constrained within rather narrow cultural boundaries. The Ukrainian girl in the story, as you can see, is breaking those constraints in a very physical way. But then she apologizes for it, of course. Utilitarian, as you say.

You ask about female characters and their sexualization. In a writing group I was in, it was once pointed out that the female characters in my story were described physically, but the males were not. I thought, okay, that's an error. That's an oversight. That's like a new Bechdel test. Did the writer provide descriptions of each gender equally, or is only one gender being sexualized? To an extent, you have to do this within the character's point of view. Is the character's point of view doing the sexualizing, or is the author doing it? And is the sexualization a flaw of the character's point of view? How are they projecting onto the other? Why do they need to do that? In this particular story, "The Stick Up," it's two women, and I would argue that the main character, Hannah, is self-sexualizing, then projecting that onto Lyudmila, the Ukrainian nanny, and Lyudmila is not having it, as the saying goes. She even makes a cynical comment that boys do nice things for her, but that just gives her power over them. But that story has a chiasmus structure, where Hannah's arc is going down, while Lyudmila's is going up. At some point, those arcs intersect, and the power is exchanged. And right as they intersect, that's when the robber comes into the coffee shop. The robbery is kind of random. Remember, I said earlier that a conflict needs that third piece? The third piece can come from left field. It often makes it more interesting when it does. So, the robber comes in, and, at that point, you have one character who is now thoroughly in power. She's chucking two thick coffee mugs at the robber. Then, she even says, "Next time, I throw three mugs." Meanwhile, Hannah is so disempowered that she literally cannot remove her wedding ring when the robber demands to have it. At that point, it's a complete reversal. Hannah gets to walk home from this situation with a very different point of view and outlook on life.

MM: I'm enamored with your endings—all your stories' endings—the way the last lines become a means to understand the story. The ending line to the final story, "Somalia," seemed to provide a metaphor for how I came to understand the entire collection. In that story, you have this gathering of old friends, married and with children together at a beach house. The men are around the fire. The women are at the water's edge with the kids. The men are having this very macho, almost cliché kind of conversation where they're chiding each other about their masculinity and their sexual prowess. Something to the effect of, "Are you going to get laid tonight with your wife?" One of the men's wives has had a relationship with one of the other men prior to their marriage. So, there's tension around that. But, at the night's end, one of the men decides to light off fireworks. I love this ending: "The rocket shot up, exploding in the air, bright as day. Lighting faces where sadness and regret and joy and wonder equally played." Amazing. What, for you, is the significance of endings? What should an ending provide for the reader? What rules, if any, do you impose upon yourself when you're composing the ending?

EMW: Well, thank you for pointing out the ending of "Somalia," because that's probably my favorite ending I've ever written. That's why I put "Somalia" at the very end of the collection. I met a woman in a writing group who had a habit of looking at the final paragraph of a story and then comparing it to the opening paragraph of the story. The idea was that there should be a thematic continuity. Not necessarily that there had to be foreshadowing, but the elements and the potentiality at the opening of the story should be recognizable all the way through to the end of the story. I love that notion. As the story works through its potentialities to settle into an inevitability, the climax of the story is a stress test of what's happened up to that point. So, for example, in the "Somalia" story where the husbands are talking on the beach, there's a lot of tension building. There's an allusion to the woman, Caroline, who may have had a relationship with the point-of-view character, David. So, things are escalating there. Then David has a soliloquy where, instead of playing along with the guys doing their performative dialogue, he breaks the mold and he lays it out in a way that becomes like a stress test for everything that's happened up to that point. To me, it's very redemptive because, clearly, he and his wife have a grounded relationship—not perfect, but it's filled with intention and commitment toward each other. That's where he lands at the end. He says, "I'm going to go up to that cabin. We're going to make love, right. And this is what you're going to do, and this is what you're going to do. And then after we make love, my wife is going to tell me all the things that the women have been saying while they were out on the sand, watching the kids play in the waves. And this is what they're going to say..." To me, it's a redemptive speech, even though it burns everything down. That's the character cashing in on all the elements that have built to that point. The only thing I don't like about that metaphor is that it's talking about money and a bank. I don't think it's the perfect metaphor. I think it's bigger than that. We get to ask, at that point, has all the imagery and potential of the story earned what's going to happen next?

MM: Which reflects the emotion of the characters, which is the important part here and throughout the collection. It's been so great talking to you about *The Divide*, Evan. Thank you.

Author **Evan Morgan Williams** is the author of four collections of short stories, most recently *The Divide*, published by Cornerstone Press, University of Wisconsin-Stevens Point (2026). He's been the recipient of several writing awards, including the Chandra Prize at BkMk Press, in addition to being long listed for the Frank O'Connor International Short Story Prize. Visit: evanmorganwilliams.com to learn more.

Interviewer **Maria McLeod**, associate professor of journalism at Western Washington University, has authored oral histories, articles, scholarly research, and creative works. Her poetry and prose have been published in literary journals in the U.S., England, Germany, India, and Scotland. She's been nominated for six Pushcart Prizes and has published two poetry chapbooks, *Mother Want*, and *Skin. Hair. Bones.*

The *Clackamas Literary Review* is typeset in Sabon LT Std, an oldstyle serif designed by Jan Tschichold, and in Optima LT Std, a humanistic sans-serif designed by Hermann Zapf, and printed on 50 lb. creme paper. Published by English Department students and faculty at Clackamas Community College, in Oregon City, Oregon.

Visit

CLR

CLACKAMAS LITERARY REVIEW

clackamasliteraryreview.org

clackamasliteraryreview.submittable.com

facebook.com/clackamasliteraryreview

@clackamaslitreview

@clackamaslitrev

Contact

clr@clackamas.edu

www.ingramcontent.com/pod-product-compliance
Lightning Source LLC
LaVergne TN
LVHW091130080826
845145LV00008B/2103
9781732033382